THE SNOW MELTED IN AUGUST

THE SNOW MELTED IN AUGUST

ALDONA MARTYNENKA

misunderstood
PRESS

First published in Sweden in 2024

ISBN (PB): 978-91-531-1166-5
ISBN (E): 978-91-531-1165-8

This is a work of fiction, however, some parts of the story are inspired by true events. In those cases, some names and characteristics have been changed, some events have been compressed, and some dialogue has been recreated. The work reflects the author's present recollections of experiences over time.

Book design and typesetting © InsideStudio26.com
Illustrations © Victoria Heath Silk

For Roma

"Death is something for a lifetime."

18.02.2013

CHAPTER 1

August 2017

Viera trembled as she struggled to catch her breath, trying to recount to me her short but exhilarating interaction with Knox, her newfound favorite artist whose existence had been unknown to us until that very day.

We stood amidst the sea of people at the festival, basking in the euphoria of the performance and still reeling from the few precious words we had managed to exchange with the tall, handsome, and unexpectedly shy musician from Estonia. Even now, Viera remained in a state of disbelief, excitement radiating from her shifty eyes and wide grin. Her childlike wonder, coupled with her dusty-rose dress that accentuated her big blue eyes, made her look like a little girl.

Viera raised her eyes at me and extended her arm, lifting her phone toward my face. I leaned over closer to the phone and squinted. As I looked at the photo on her phone, I couldn't help but admit that she and Knox looked cute together.

"I promise, your husband will never know how excited you were after taking a photo with this random man," I teased with a grin.

"He is not a ran… Oh, stop, Janina!" Her cheeks flushed, and then she broke into a cheerful laugh.

It had been an incredible day, and my heart pounded with happiness. I hadn't felt this way in a long time. With everything going on with Raman, his addiction and a few overdoses, the past few months had felt like a never-ending descent into darkness, with no glimmer of hope. But now, with Raman sober and me being back in Miensk with my best friend by my side, things were finally falling into place. I felt lucky and happy, marveling at how the universe always seemed to put everything in place.

As we pushed through the crowd, I screamed in Viera's ear how happy I was, but she couldn't hear me. We laughed and hurried out of the stifling atmosphere of the dance floor, eager to talk.

Stepping away from the crowd, I took a deep breath, relishing the crispness of the fresh air. Together, we headed toward the coffee tent, my heart still racing from the thrill of the day.

Just then, my phone buzzed with a text message from Natasha.

>

Call me when you have someone with you

Boom. Boom. Boom.

In the sudden silence around me, I could only hear the steady thud of my own heart. Dread clawed at my insides. It had to be about Raman. No, no, no. Please, no.

I looked at Viera, who had stopped laughing and was staring at me with a perplexed expression. My blood ran cold as I called Natasha back.

"Hello." Natasha's voice sounded raspy, as if she hadn't spoken in a while. For a second, I stopped breathing, waiting for her to speak. "Janina, are you with someone right now?"

"Yes!" I shouted. "Natasha, what happened?" I asked, bracing myself for the worst.

"Raman is dead."

CHAPTER 2

August 2008

I was abruptly jolted awake by the bus's sudden stop. Blinking groggily, I tried to recall the dream I had just been in, but it eluded me. I glanced at my dad, but he was too engrossed in conversation with another passenger to notice me. Dad's brown, graying curls swayed in rhythm with his animated gestures as he passionately exchanged thoughts with the man seated opposite us, trying to keep his voice down. I sighed, feeling frustrated.

Looking out the window, I saw rows of old, two-story apartment buildings and narrow, crowded streets filled with cars and people dressed in dull, monotonous clothing. I pressed my face to the glass, trying to catch a glimpse of the sky, but it was impossible to tell if it was cloudy or not. Everyone looked so gloomy here.

I attempted to turn in my seat to stretch my legs, but my knees already pressed firmly against the backrest of the seat in front, a constant reminder of busses being designed for much shorter passengers than me.

When would this journey end? I longed to get off the bus and stretch my body on a soft hotel bed with fresh, crisp sheets. I smiled at the thought, but my morning crankiness prevented me from fully anticipating the exciting things to come this weekend.

Speaking of which, the reason for this weekend's excitement lay ahead. My father, a locally renowned music journalist, managed to pull me into this festival trip to Lviv, Ukraine, by marking me as a supporting journalist. To be clear, I was far from being a journalist. Dad managed to get away with this only because his close friend Ryhor Kureichyk organized the festival. My personal plan for the weekend, in turn, was enjoying the festival and the chance to see the Rockets, my favorite band. Would Raman, one of the band's members, recognize me if I went up to say hello? He must remember me from when my dad introduced me to the band a while ago. Probably not, I thought, sighing.

The memory of that day vividly reappeared before my eyes. I was a skinny teenager, dressed in wide blue jeans that dragged over my white Adidas Superstars, and an oversized hoodie. Dark brown bangs hung over my eyes, and my arms were covered with friendship bracelets and festival armbands.

My classmate and I were at a festival in a park in Miensk to help my dad and Kureichyk sell CDs and books. We stood by the merch tent, waiting for Dad to give us instructions, when a tall, bony guy with long black bangs hanging over one side of his face approached us, asking for Kureichyk.

Dad looked up from the large bag on the ground and exclaimed, "Hello, Raman! What a pleasure to see you!" He extended his hand to him.

The guy greeted Dad with a smile and shook his hand.

Turning to us, Dad wrapped his arm around the guy's shoulder and said, "Girls, I'm pleased to introduce Raman Krasouski to you. The most talented musician you can possibly find in Belarus."

Raman laughed cheerfully, his deep laughter echoing in my head. "I wish I had your optimism about that."

"You should! You really are talented, Raman."

Raman smiled in response.

"This is my daughter, by the way!" Dad said, pointing at me.

"Hi," I mumbled.

"She is the most dedicated Rockets fan. You should see her running around the house every morning blasting your songs and singing along."

"Dad, stop!" I wished I could sink into the ground.

Raman smiled and asked, "Then come to our next show?"

"Yeah, I…"

"Oh, she definitely will!" Dad's loud voice cut me off.

After getting the information about Kureichyk's location, Raman thanked us and left. I watched him disappear into the crowd, feeling a barely noticeable fluttering in my chest. I swallowed, suddenly scared of the growing excitement and unsure of what to do with it.

From that day on, I became the biggest Rockets fan. I collected the band's photos in a special folder on my computer, printed pictures of Raman, and stuck them on my walls alongside other celebrities. I listened to their songs non-stop and attended every single show in my city. Finally, my life had meaning.

Returning to the present, stuck on the shaking bus, I giggled, reminiscing about the child I was back then.

I looked out of the window at the buildings we were passing by. Abandonment and poverty screamed from every corner, but as we drove further into the city, I couldn't help but fall in love with it. The crumbling buildings and abandoned shops exuded a unique charm that fascinated me. The character of this place was captivating, and my excitement began to grow.

The bus stopped again, and I turned to my dad to ask if this was our stop. But the confused expression on his face told me he didn't know either. The noise level on the bus rose as people started talking and trying to figure out what was going on. Suddenly, the door creaked open, and the driver stepped out.

My heart skipped a beat when I saw Ales and a few other musicians from the Rockets standing next to their van, explaining something to the bus driver. It was only when one of them turned, revealing his profile, that I recognized Raman among them. His lips moved slowly as he addressed the driver, his long, slender fingers firmly gripped the man's shoulder. He fixed the driver with an intense gaze, a mischievous grin playing across his lips.

My legs trembled with fear, and I sank back into my seat. What should I do? Should I try to talk to them?

As the bus filled with noise, some people getting up from their seats and others just shouting over each other, I heard the door click shut, and the engine started. The bus moved away from the band.

"Shit. Shit, shit, shit!" I muttered under my breath. It would have been such a great chance to talk if they joined us on the bus. Although… Who am I lying to? No way I'd come to them and start a conversation. I'd just sit in my fucking seat and secretly envy their joy. I crossed my arms over my chest and pouted.

"How's your mood?" Dad patted my knee, trying to start a conversation.

"It's okay," I answered and turned away to the window.

He turned his attention back to the previous interlocutors, and the rest of the way I spent in silence, lost in my own thoughts.

I was grateful that instead of the usual "let me cheer you up," Dad gave me space. I definitely didn't feel like talking about my feelings with him. I wondered if others had similar relationships with their fathers. I always felt like my dad was more of a fun friend to hang out with rather than a traditional father figure. And, to be honest, I loved that because I could brag to my friends about how we went to concerts and festivals together while their dads were boring office clerks.

O

After what seemed like an eternity, we finally arrived at the hotel. The moment I stepped off the bus, I was in awe of the massive building in front of me. Enormous wooden doors led us right into the round hallway with a sparkling crystal chandelier. I stood in the middle of the hallway, feeling myself a grain of sand in this majesty.

As Dad went straight to the reception to check us in, I put my bag down and stared up at the ceiling. A woman, who I assumed was a housekeeper, approached me.

"It took almost forty years for the king's servants to hand-paint this," she said, pointing up at the intricate designs on the ceiling. "Imagine climbing up the ladder every day for four decades and drawing this again and again?"

She seemed to be in her fifties, a small woman barely reaching my shoulder, with a kind smile on her face. She was looking at me, awaiting a reaction as if it was the first time she had ever told anyone this secret.

"This sounds absolutely crazy… Almost forty years," I replied.

"Almost forty years," she echoed and walked away.

Dad returned with the room keys, interrupting my thoughts.

"It's on the third floor. We've got a room for just us two," he said, handing me the papers and keys.

"Yaaay! The whole room for us?"

"Yes, you should thank Kureichyk when you see him," Dad said with a smile.

"Uh-huh." I picked up my bag from the floor and followed Dad. "Did you know that some guy was hand-painting this stuff on the ceiling for like forty years?"

"Yeah?" He looked up for a moment without stopping.

We climbed the old circular stairs; the carpet muffling our footsteps. After passing a few white wooden doors, we reached our room.

I turned the key in the lock and entered the room, greeted by the pleasant yellow light of sunrise. The space was huge, with old wooden furniture, three single beds, and a high ceiling. I opened the bathroom door and couldn't hold back my "Ah!"

"Is it that good?" Dad peeked over my shoulder. "Yeah, it could be worse."

I laughed. "Worse? It looks like a palace! Look at the bathtub!" I exclaimed.

"What do you need from a bathtub? Just some water, huh?" Dad joked.

I rolled my eyes and shut the door. Dad put his bag on one of the beds and started taking things out of it, muttering under his breath. I walked to the bed by the balcony and started unpacking, too.

"I have to rush there now to set up a tent and stuff. Are you joining me?"

I hesitated, feeling the pit in my stomach. The last time I ate was back in Miensk yesterday evening.

"Uhm, now? Do you think we'll have food there?" I asked, hoping he had brought some snacks.

"I don't know!" he answered impatiently. "Janina, we shouldn't expect everything to be fixed for us. We should be grateful for what we have."

His words made me feel uneasy, but I remained silent.

Seeing the disappointment on my face, he added, "We'll grab

something on the way. Daddy won't leave his kiddo hungry." He chuckled, and I forced a smile.

"I need to shower and change, and then I'm ready to go," I said, eager to break the tension.

When I returned to the room after my shower, my dad was nowhere to be seen. The balcony door was open, and the humid air of the rainy city wafted in. I poked my head out and saw the asphalt below was slick with rain, and the scent of wet soil filled my nostrils. For a moment, I was transported to a forest, and an overwhelming urge to escape came over me.

I sat down on the bed, letting my shoulders slump and arching my back. What are you doing here, Janina? I wondered.

The curtain rustled, and I got up to close the balcony door. As I did, I caught a glimpse of my dad standing below it, smoking. He was glancing around nervously, unaware that I could see him. He probably didn't realize our balcony was on this side, and I could easily see him doing this *obscenity*.

I grabbed a gray hoodie and a clean pair of black jeans and quickly dressed. A light touch of black eyeliner to accentuate my dark eyes, and I was ready to go.

As I stepped outside, I found Dad already finished with his cigarette, standing tall, with his hands tucked in the pockets of his denim jacket. Admiring his casual yet fashionable outfit consisting of a blue t-shirt with the festival's logo, a loose denim jacket with patches from various rock bands and festivals, blue jeans, and classic white Nikes, I couldn't help but wonder why I ever felt embarrassed by his appearance. My laughter echoed in response to my thoughts, and he joined in, too.

"You look beautiful," he complimented me.

"Thank you, you do too."

"We should take a picture together by this building!" he said, wrapping his arm around my bony shoulders and turning me around to show what he meant. I shrugged, and he rushed to a passerby, asking them to take a picture.

Gazing at the photo on his old-school digital camera, my dad's eyes diverted somewhere behind me.

"Shit!" he suddenly exclaimed and dashed toward the tram stop.

Hastily, I followed him and jumped into the tram as he held the doors open for me.

As I panted, trying to catch my breath, he teased me, "We didn't raise you to be this weak!"

I rolled my eyes and plopped down onto a seat next to him. He landed by my side and asked, "Will you be able to help us with the merch?"

"Yeah," I answered, wiping my forehead with my hoodie's sleeve.

Just a few minutes later, we arrived at the park's entrance, where a colossal monument towered overhead. As we walked past it, I suddenly felt like it was toppling over. Rushing forward to keep pace with my dad, I couldn't help but glance back at the sculpture, half-expecting it to crumble. My heart pounded in my chest, and I struggled to catch my breath.

As we made our way into the festival area, my spirits lifted at the sight of musicians milling about, tuning their instruments or relaxing with a cold beer. However, my excitement was short-lived when I spotted a stack of t-shirts I had to sell in a nearby tent. I realized I wouldn't have a moment to catch any of the shows.

My frustration boiled over as I caught sight of Kureichyk's short and stout figure, strutting around, barking orders with his rotund belly straining against his belt, sweat beading on his bald head.

When he noticed us, he flashed a lazy smile, shaking hands with my dad before gesturing toward the tent filled with CDs and books. "Are these up to snuff?" he asked.

"Of course, Ryhor! They're perfect!" Dad replied, carrying bags of merchandise to the tent to start setting up.

Kureichyk then turned to me, his yellow teeth bared in a sickly smile.

"Can you handle selling the t-shirts?" he asked me, nodding toward the heap of blue and yellow garments on the table.

"Sure," I muttered, dragging my feet toward the tent.

Annoyance prickled in my throat—annoyance with myself for having such unrealistic expectations. Did I really think they'd take me to a festival for free without expecting anything in return?

Sorting the shirts by size, I felt a lump rising in my throat. I felt foolish. But I couldn't dwell on it for long. The doors opened, and a throng of people swarmed the tent, bombarding me with questions about the merchandise. I was so busy trying to keep up with demand, searching for the right size, and collecting cash that I lost track of time. Hours flew by until Ryhor finally interrupted me.

"Hey, go eat some lunch," he said, grabbing my elbow. "Count the money and keep 10% for yourself."

"Yeah?"

He smiled and walked away.

Wow, this is going to be more than just one lunch, I thought, looking down at my pockets overflowing with cash. I hadn't expected to get paid for this.

Not wanting to leave my dad alone for too long, I hurried to McDonald's, grabbed a burger, and quickly returned. I sat down on the curb behind the stage and began to eat.

Suddenly, out of nowhere, Ales appeared and sat next to me. I looked at him, stunned, and he smiled, saying "Hi, Janina."

He fixed me with a mocking gaze, his piercing blue eyes betraying an impending smirk. A snug navy t-shirt accentuated his muscular shoulders. Although his lips remained motionless, the hint of a grin lurked beneath the surface. His usual bluntness, seemingly crafted to unsettle and undermine any interaction, never failed to catch me off-guard. It fueled a constant unease in me, fearing his next remark would leave me speechless. As I met his unwavering gaze, perspiration gathered above my lips.

I must have looked surprised because he laughed before I could respond. I mumbled a greeting while trying to chew my burger as fast as possible.

As I was thinking of what to say to him, I heard a camera shutter and turned my head in that direction. A tall guy in a khaki hoodie stood next to us with his face behind the camera. I smiled, and he raised his thumb, approving the photo before leaving.

Once again, Ales and I were alone. I quietly chewed my burger, hoping he would either start a conversation or leave. I couldn't understand why he kept sitting there, and I was too nervous to look at him. I kept staring ahead, slowly chewing my food, as if that was a valid enough reason for my silence.

"How are you doing, Janina?" he finally asked.

"I'm good," I quickly replied, still avoiding eye contact.

He stood up, looked down at me with a grin, and walked away. As I watched him walk away, I felt a growing hatred toward myself. Why was I always so awkward in these situations? I grew up in this environment but still couldn't seem to feel comfortable around musicians.

My thoughts were interrupted when I noticed a familiar face among the group of people Ales walked to. It was Raman. Tall, with dark hair and long bangs, wearing a pink hoodie with the hood up, yellow sunglasses, skinny jeans, and… with a girl wrapped in his arms. I gulped.

I suddenly wished I could disappear and be back home in Miensk, in my room. I didn't want to believe he had a girlfriend.

What else did you expect, Janina? You couldn't even talk to Ales when he approached you! You're so stupid! Raman will never even notice someone like you! You're invisible to him! You're so miserable...

O

I woke up alone in the hotel room. The bed next to mine was made, and the bathroom door was open with no light inside. I wondered why Dad hadn't woken me up to go with him.

I stretched in my bed and smiled as I realized I had some unexpected free time to explore the city on my own. I desperately needed some alone time, and this was the perfect opportunity.

As the sun rose, I got out of bed and stared at myself in the mirror for a moment, wondering if I was pretty enough or attractive enough for someone like Raman to notice me. Shaking the thought away, I dug through my clothes and found yesterday's jeans. To my surprise, I discovered some more money from yesterday's sales, and I couldn't help but let out an evil laugh. Today was shaping up to be a good day.

After a quick shower, I made my way out of the hotel. The humid air immediately clung to my curly hair, and I couldn't help but worry about what it would look like by the time the Rockets began their performance. The gathering clouds didn't offer much hope, but thankfully, I had the foresight to bring a hoodie along.

As I fumbled through my bag searching for a hair tie, I reminded myself to take a deep breath and enjoy the moment. I was in the most beautiful city in the world, and there was no sense in wasting my time fretting about my hair. With no specific destination in mind, I embarked on my journey.

The bustling streets were teeming with people enjoying their Sunday morning, dining on the terraces of cafés, and taking leisurely strolls. It was invigorating to be surrounded by so much activity, yet to feel completely anonymous at the same time. No one knew me and no one cared.

A white sign depicting a cup caught my eye, and I knew I had to have a cup of coffee. The doorbell jingled as I entered the cozy cafe, and I was greeted with a warm smile from the barista.

Ordering my coffee, I then took a seat by the window and gazed out at the street. I fluttered, anticipating the day. I felt at ease. The space embraced me with the quiet murmuring of chatter, and I couldn't wish for more.

I lost myself in the dreams when I heard a saucer and a cup clinking when the barista put them on the table. I winced, and the guy smiled, apologizing for scaring me. I smiled, looking at his friendly face. Long, sun-streaked hair and tanned skin made him look like a surfer. He apologized again and walked away.

I blushed, still thinking about the barista's smile as I sipped the coffee. The foam was thick and creamy, with just a hint of bitterness. The warmth and tranquility of the café made me feel at ease, without any need to rush.

I thought about how anxious I'd felt in the last few weeks before coming here. I realized how much the change of scenery had affected my mood. Watching the people pass by, I wondered what they were going through in their daily lives. They must have struggles too, right? What are they anxious about? Do they feel lonely?

I often felt lonely. I often thought about this heavy longing that I felt almost every day. A dull, bug-like, sticky numbness of my existence. How I often looked around, trying to break free. To be able to live and enjoy life. No matter how good things were, I was always dead inside. Sometimes I felt like it was just who I was and nothing and no one could make me feel differently.

I sighed deeply and left the café with a heavy heart. I didn't feel excited about the festival anymore and wanted to walk until my feet screamed. Passing through the old town and a sculpture park, I caught the rain and continued walking until I stumbled upon a grassy hill. Despite the wetness, I lay down and breathed in the fresh, humid air. I was starting to feel at peace again. However, my tranquility didn't last long.

When I tried to find my way back to the park for the Rockets' show, I realized I had gone too far from the city center. My heart raced as I looked around, feeling lost and alone. I had no map and was too shy to talk to strangers. I tried to remember what the park was called, but I couldn't. The only characteristic I remembered clearly was that it was located on a big hill. I started moving up the street because it made perfect sense to me until I reached the top and realized that I was way too far from the city center.

My heart was trembling, my hoodie was wet from sweat after the long climb up. I looked around and burst into tears. I fucked up. Everything was falling apart. I came here specifically to meet Raman, and now I was in the middle of fucking nowhere. Alone and broken.

As I walked back to the city, I felt defeated and empty. The show had already started, and I had missed my chance. All I wanted was to teleport back to my hotel room, crawl into bed, and forget about the day.

After a while, I caught sight of the same tram Dad and I had taken on our first visit to the park. Jumping aboard, I settled by the window and let out a deep breath, feeling a sense of security wash over me.

It took almost an hour to arrive at the park, and I was surprised to find myself completely disoriented. I must have wandered quite far.

Exiting the tram, I made a beeline for the festival bus. With nightfall upon us, I had no interest in trudging up the endless flight of stairs leading to the event. Settling into my seat, I shut my eyes for just a moment and promptly dozed off.

I awoke to someone vigorously shaking my shoulder. Blinking blearily, I looked up at the man trying to rouse me. He glared at me, bellowing, "Wake up!"

"I'm up, I'm up..." I muttered irritably.

He fell silent for a beat, waiting for me to regain consciousness.

"What happened?" I demanded, hardly in the mood to be polite.

"Your father has been searching for you all night! You scared the shit out of him!" he replied.

"What do you mean? I'm right here!" I protested.

"He thought he had lost you! Why are you putting him through this?" The man sighed deeply, then walked to the door and stuck his head out, bellowing to someone, "She's here!"

Within moments, Dad had boarded the bus, looking strange. He wasn't shouting or berating me as I expected. Instead, he wore an uncharacteristically subdued expression, though he was smiling slightly.

"I'm so glad I found you," he said, his voice soft. "I was really worried, you know. But it's alright, I'm okay now."

I stared at him, unsure of what to say.

The man who had woken me up pushed past my father, standing directly behind him. "You need to be tougher on her. This behavior is unacceptable," he snapped. "Do you even comprehend how he must have felt, thinking he had lost his child in an unfamiliar city?"

I had no response. I gazed at the two of them, perplexed. The compassion in Dad's eyes nearly moved me to tears, and I wanted nothing more than to embrace him, to reassure him that he was safe. I couldn't shake the thought of what my mother's reaction would be if she discovered that her ex-husband had managed to lose their daughter on their very first trip together in a new city.

That night, as the bus was returning to Miensk, we traveled into a pitch-black void. The inside of the bus was equally dim, and the passengers had all grown silent. Gone were the carefree strolls between seats, the chitchat, and laughter. My feet ached, and I longed to remove my shoes and stretch out my legs. My mind was worn out from the day's setbacks. Letting out a deep sigh of frustration, I closed my eyes once more.

The next morning, I awoke in my bed, in a dimly lit and chilly room. The lights flickered on the frosted glass door to my room, and the kitchen was silent.

Carefully, I crawled out of bed and wrapped myself in a blanket, then tiptoed to the study. After turning on the computer, I pulled the blanket up to my chin, shivering as I waited for it to load.

As soon as the screen illuminated, I opened the browser and clicked on the Facebook icon. That's when I noticed Ales from the Rockets was online. Without hesitation, I sent him a "What's up?" message and held my breath, waiting for a response.

He read my message and replied within a matter of seconds.

>
Thank God, you're found.

I stared at the screen for a moment, unsure of what he meant.
"Daaaaad?" I called out.
"What?" He peeked his head through the doorway.
I read Ales's message out loud.

"Well, I had to go on stage and ask everyone if they had seen you."

I turned my head to him in shock.

He came closer and added, "What? I was worried."

Oh, dear. I swallowed. Now everyone at the festival would remember me as a clueless teenager who got lost in a new city.

CHAPTER 3

August 2017

The excruciating pain in my stomach felt like a knife piercing through me, tearing me apart from the inside. I took a deep breath.

"What?" I asked Natasha, trying to sound normal.

"You heard me," she replied calmly.

"But how do you know that?" I asked, still in disbelief.

"Pasha read it in their Facebook group."

"I have to go," I blurted out, trying to hang up before Natasha could say anything else.

"Janina…"

I couldn't believe it was true. I repeated this to myself as I fought back tears, determined to verify the information.

Viera's blue eyes were fixed on me, demanding an answer. "What did she say?" she asked.

"She said Raman died." I nervously giggled, realizing how ridiculous it sounded. "I mean, this can't be true. I'll double-check. She mentioned it was on Facebook," I said, trying to ignore the tears welling up in Viera's eyes.

"What?" Her tone remained calm, unchanged.

"This must have been a mistake. Don't worry," I reassured her, even though my own mind raced to make sense of it. I refused to believe this was true. I urged myself not to cry, but the tears still came.

In just a few seconds, I found the post.

Today, our dear friend and fellow member of the NPL band Raman Krasouski has passed away. May he rest in peace.

It was like another punch in the gut. At first, I felt nothing. But then, a wave of emotions hit me like a ton of bricks. The weight of everything that had happened in the last few months just landed on my chest, and I burst into tears. Tears upon tears. My brain stubbornly tried to find a logical explanation for this, but it didn't work. The facts didn't come together.

I looked around at the people passing by, wondering how they could go about their day as if nothing had happened while Raman was dead. It was suffocating. My head felt empty. *Has passed away.* Raman…

"I need to go home. Can you call a cab for me?" I asked Viera, handing her my phone.

Tears kept streaming down my face and my hands shook. Viera's cheeks glimmered with tears as well. I knew she was afraid to speak or even touch me.

"Of course," she whispered.

After Viera called a cab for me, we walked in silence to the parking lot. We shared a brief hug before I got into the car. Closing the door, I exhaled deeply, hoping the driver wouldn't ask any questions.

Surprisingly, I didn't cry during the ride. My only escape from the overwhelming pain was to think logically and plan my next steps. I needed to talk to someone who could confirm this was all a mistake. Raman couldn't have died. I just needed some proof.

Suddenly, I thought of Ales. Why hadn't he helped? He was always so loud and engaged in political and public matters, yet when his friend was on the brink of death, he didn't do anything at all. He could have influenced Raman, could have prevented this tragedy.

Anger boiled up inside me, directed at everyone who was a part of it, everyone who didn't help, everyone around me. Most of all, I hated myself.

No, it must have been a mistake. Maybe it was just a post on Facebook, a sick joke. I had to know for sure.

Without thinking of the consequences, I messaged Katsia. Everything was going to be alright. She would find it out and tell me it wasn't true.

<

Is it true about Raman?

>

What?

<

Pasha said he died

They posted on Facebook

I waited anxiously for her reply, hoping against hope that she would tell me it was all a hoax.

I wasn't even thinking she might not know about it. And I just told her that her close friend had died. No mercy. No thinking about her feelings.

Suddenly, I felt a pang of regret for throwing it out at her so abruptly. She cared about him, even though she tried to hide it.

I couldn't shake the sorrow at the thought of her dealing with another drug addict, especially with her father already struggling with heroin. All this shit with her family, her own battles, and her boyfriend Siargei's descent into addiction together with Raman, weighed heavily on my mind. I shuddered, brushing off the thought. Raman would pull through just fine.

A few minutes later, Katsia messaged me back.

>

It's true

Another wave of panic washed over me. God, God, God… Why? Please, someone, tell me it's not true. Bullshit. Please, no, no, please, for God's sake!

I held my breath for a moment. I couldn't break down in a cab. I needed to get home first.

Just then, my phone vibrated with another message. I felt a flicker of hope. Maybe someone else would tell me it was all a lie. I glanced at the screen.

>

Will you come to the funeral?

"Daaaaaamn," I muttered, feeling a surge of anger and frustration. I took a deep breath and tried to calm myself down. This was not the time to lose it.

<

*I'd like to, but I'm afraid his family is not
really looking forward to seeing us*

The thought of Raman lying in a coffin, lifeless and still,

sent a chill down my spine. I forced myself to take another deep breath and focus on the conversation. Breathe out.

<

Where's the funeral? In Mahilyow?

> *I think his dad would like to see us*
>
> *And I don't know yet*
>
> *I'll text you tomorrow*

The anger and frustration bubbled up inside me again. "Fuck, it's true, it's true," I muttered to myself. Raman, you piece of shit. How could you do this to us? I had no doubts it was an overdose. And I hated him for that.

<

Do you know what happened?

Overdose?

> *Yes*

Fuck.

> *Your friend was right*
>
> *About August*
>
> *Damn*
>
> *I couldn't believe it until the very end*

I put my phone in my pocket and hastily stepped out of the car. I rushed to the door and opened it with a creak. I pressed the elevator button and fidgeted while waiting for it to arrive. As soon as it did, I quickly entered and pressed the button for my floor. I bolted toward my front door, fumbling for the key in my pocket. With trembling hands, I finally managed to fit the key into the lock and turn it.

As I stepped into the corridor, my voice quivered as I muttered, "Mom…" My emotions overwhelmed me, and tears erupted.

"What?" she called from her bedroom, unaware that something terrible had happened.

"M-m-mom…"

Her chair creaked as she pushed it back. The thudding of her feet on the carpet filled the narrow space of the hallway. She was running toward me, concern etched on her face.

"What's going on? What happened?" Her eyes were wide open with fear as she frantically searched for an answer. She probably assumed that something terrible had happened to me.

I wished that was the case.

CHAPTER 4

March 2010–July 2013

Raman reappeared in my life just two years later, during a period of significant change. I had started my university studies, landed a decent job, and found myself in a relationship with a man who brought stability and a sense of contentment to my life. The kind of guy who was safe and made me feel like I was doing fine with my life. At least, that was what it appeared on the surface.

Deep down, I felt like I was drowning, suffocating under the weight of disappointment and frustration that seemed to permeate my existence. I yearned to break free, to do something crazy and exciting, to be with someone exciting. Instead, I found myself trapped in a mundane life I couldn't see myself living. I made desperate attempts to escape this emotional quicksand but nothing seemed to alleviate this unease within me.

Then, one day, I saw a girl on the street walking with crutches. She had only one leg. I gazed at her and couldn't help but ask myself, what right do I have to complain about my life? I had everything. My body worked, my brain worked. I had a family, friends, a boyfriend, a job—everything. On the surface, I seemed perfectly fine, but the truth was far from it. The realization struck me like a thunderbolt, and I couldn't hold back the tears. No, I wasn't fine at all.

With these thoughts floating in my head, I entered the elevator at my university. I chose to stand in the corner, facing the wall, instead of engaging with the people around me, as was my habit. Predictably, the elevator was crowded, and everyone seemed to be headed to the top floor. 11, 12, 13, 14, and that was my cue.

Stepping out of the elevator, I offered a wave to my classmates but felt an unexplainable sense of unwelcome among them. I kept walking to the big windowsill by the classroom, where a few girls from my group were gathered.

"Hey, guys," I uttered softly as I effortlessly slipped between bags and notebooks lying on the windowsill. Sitting there somehow spared me the ordeal of facing my classmates head-on, allowing me a temporary reprieve from social interaction.

"Oh, hi, Janina!" chimed in the dark-haired girl, her gaze shifting toward me as she moved closer. "How was your weekend?"

"Um, it was alright. I brought a dog from a shelter to my boyfriend's place, so we spent the weekend hanging with the doggo." I managed a grin. "How about you?"

"That's so nice! I love dogs! My husband and I won't have time for anything else except the baby! So busy every moment! And I have to study as well… You know…"

"Yeah, totally," I replied, silently hoping she'd return to whatever she was occupied with before I arrived. This conversation made me feel uneasy.

Suddenly, my eyes caught sight of Alena across the hallway. A wave of relief washed over me, and without a second thought, I jumped off the windowsill.

As I approached Alena, she greeted me warmly with a smile. We exchanged hugs and caught up on life. She had been busy with school, trying to graduate ahead of schedule.

We walked back toward the windowsill. The girls were already talking about something that I didn't care about enough to listen to, but then my thoughts stopped for a moment when I heard something familiar.

"I don't personally know the guy, but I've heard he's an amazing tattoo artist. You just have to go to Mahilyow," someone mentioned. My heart skipped a beat, and I held my breath.

"I wouldn't trust some random guy, especially in Mahilyow. Come on, find a normal artist, Aksana." The short girl with red hair chuckled.

Unable to resist, I asked, "What's the name of the artist?"

"Raman UFO. You know him?"

Alena and I exchanged glances. I figured that being from Mahilyow, Alena probably knew Raman quite well.

"Yeah, a bit," I cautiously admitted. All eyes immediately turned toward me, filled with curiosity. "Well, it's not that exciting," I began, as if I needed to justify my connection. "I met him when I was around 14. My dad introduced us."

"Is he as wild as they say? What is he like as a person? He's so hot! Oh my God! And his arms, all covered with tattoos… OMG, he's so fucking hot!" Her eyebrows danced upward, while her chin emphasized each word with a subtle nod forward. "Does he ever visit Miensk?"

The barrage of questions overwhelmed me, and unfortunately, I didn't have all the answers. Nonetheless, my classmates were clearly impressed, and it felt good.

After class, I bid a quick farewell to everyone and slipped into the elevator before it got crowded. I was buzzing with excitement at what had happened. Glancing at my reflection in the elevator mirror, I pondered what might happen if I reached out to him. Surely, he must remember my name, right?

I came up with some ridiculous reason to message him and asked about tattoos. To my surprise, he responded, and to my even greater astonishment, his reply was longer and warmer than I had expected. We managed to sustain a conversation through a few messages, after which I gave up. He was actively replying and was incredibly nice, but I saw he wasn't interested. In fact, I wasn't even sure if he recognized who I was.

O

Several years later, the universe had given me another chance to reconnect with Raman. At this point, I was employed at a small bank in Miensk. My life hadn't miraculously transformed into unbridled happiness, but at least I had a job that I found some solace in. I may not have become a happier person overall, but for a few hours each day, I felt so.

Within the confines of this same bank, or more precisely, within the work network, I struck up conversations with a colleague stationed at our branch office in Mahilyow. Natasha and I did the same job in different cities and always had things to talk about. I admired her wisdom and self-assurance. Natasha exuded a sense of calm that put me at ease, and she always had answers to my worries.

We connected pretty well and could talk about anything. As time passed, we discovered that we shared a multitude of mutual friends. In passing, I mentioned how crazy I was about the Rockets, without specifying about whom in particular. It was Natasha who casually brought up Raman, mainly because she wasn't familiar with the others in the band. I was shocked. She knew him.

She told me about the things going on in Raman's life, mentioning his collaboration with the renowned rapper Labs. Quite a big break. She asked me if I knew Raman well, and for some reason, I found myself lying. I pretended to be more interested in Ales. I was too shy to confess my puppy love for Raman. Of course, I didn't know him well, but I felt like I did. My heart raced, and I couldn't understand why.

Natasha also shared that Raman had quit drugs. He distanced himself from his junkie friends and spent days at home writing music for Labs. I remembered how I tried to hide my enthusiasm, continuing the conversation by awkwardly jesting about Labs' inability to even write music by himself. To which Natasha just replied that she hoped Raman cleaned up his act.

Later that evening, I lay on a makeshift mattress in my half-empty room, browsing Raman's Facebook profile. I stumbled upon a link to his Twitter account, where his last post read, "Death is something for a lifetime."

I closed my laptop and stared at the ceiling. Raman scared me, but it only made me want him more. His whole personality had an irresistible pull, like a magnet, fueled by the thrill, the danger, and the fun. I yearned to be near him.

I sighed. The situation felt surreal, yet thanks to Natasha, I harbored hope that I might have a chance to connect with Raman.

The following day, I learned that Raman started working with Astap, an even bigger figure in the music industry, and was going on tour with him. My hope waned. He became a too big star for me.

O

Within a few months of chatting online at work, Natasha extended a surprising invitation for me to visit her in Mahilyow.

Even though it was an unexpected invitation given how little we knew each other, I forced myself to accept it and went on a weekend trip to her city.

It was my first time in Mahilyow, and I immediately fell in love with the city, despite the grayness of its character that permeated everything—from the weather to the architecture, even down to the attire and expressions of its inhabitants. The only glimmers of vibrancy in the city came from the never-ending advertisements thrown out at every wall and billboard. Everything else was gray and dark, and I immediately fell for it.

As I discovered later, among locals, Mahilyow bore the nickname "Mahila," translating from Belarusian as "grave." It wasn't surprising that the city became a fertile ground for the Belarusian underground culture, nurturing a wealth of talented artists and musicians who found inspiration amidst its solemn ambiance.

As I spent more time with Natasha in person, I could see more and more how strikingly beautiful she was. She had a doll-like face, a gracefully curvaceous figure, and exuded a maternal warmth that enveloped those around her. Her flawless, glossy hair and classic makeup gave her the appearance of a magazine cover model. Natasha effortlessly commanded attention from every man around her but she had already made her choice. Since the age of 19, she'd been together with her boyfriend Pasha and couldn't care less about other men.

Pasha, in turn, was very *normal*. Working at a local bar called Cuba and lacking any standout talents or physical features, he possessed a remarkable gift for making everyone feel at ease in his presence. He prioritized others' comfort over his own ego, willingly making himself the butt of jokes to ensure nobody felt out of place. Pasha was akin to a comforting blanket, enveloping those around him with his warmth. And the biggest part of Pasha was Natasha. He looked at her with the adoration of a loyal puppy, incapable of envisioning his life without her by his side.

Since that initial visit, spending time with Natasha and Pasha in their Mahilyow apartment had become a refuge of calm and solace for me.

CHAPTER 5

August 2017

I lay in my bed, howling and gripped by anguish. My jaw clenched the corner of the pillow so tightly that I could hear the faint rattle of my teeth. My gaze fixated, unblinking, on the empty space before me. My eyes stung with tears, and I closed them, letting two lines of tears run down my burning cheeks. I shuddered uncontrollably, a numbness coursing through me.

Mom tried to calm me down, but I didn't hear anything except her rambling. All I could think about was the reality of Raman's death. He was gone.

"I hate him!" The words erupted from my lips, the only coherent expression of my pain. "I hate him so much…"

"Come on, you shouldn't say that," my mother implored, her voice attempting to bring reason to my grief. "It's not his fault. Raman struggled with health issues, but he fought hard to overcome them, didn't he? Perhaps it was simply his fate. It's not his fault, Janina."

"He overdosed! This isn't about health problems, Mom. He's the one guilty, the only one! I tried… I tried. I hate him so much…"

I was gasping for air, but each breath felt like fire scorching my throat as soon as it touched it. As if I'd just swallowed a piece of burning coal.

Amidst my despair, I heard the notification sounds on my phone, each one like a cruel reminder of the world continuing to turn. I leaped out of bed, wiping away the tears, and squinted at the screen through blurry vision. I prayed for a message that would prove it was all a mistake—a denial from Katsia or news from Siargei that they had spoken to Mikola and Raman, proving it false.

I scrolled through the notifications, trembling hands clutching the phone. My vision remained clouded, my eyes raw from the onslaught of tears. Where is it? What are these stupid messages and Instagram likes? Who fucking cares?

> *Hi, sorry for your loss.*
>
> *You've done everything you could.*

Noooooo… No, no, no, this isn't what I'm after.

> *Baby, I'm so sorry…*

Jesus, how did even Nasta find out? Why is everyone already aware? What if it's not even true?

I collapsed onto the bed and curled up. No tears left, nor any ability to speak.

Mom gently stroked my head and asked, "Was he just a friend, or was there more?"

I glanced up for a second, my gaze frozen. A moment later, I closed my eyes and howled over again.

Several hours later, my mom, after repeatedly asking if I'd be okay alone, finally decided to retire to her own bed.

"Yes, Mom, yes," I assured her.

I watched her silhouette approach the door and flick off the light. She lingered for a few moments in the doorway, her petite and shapely figure stark against the brightness behind her, then silently closed the door, casting my room into darkness.

I rolled over and stared at the ceiling. The pain had dissipated, leaving me empty. I felt relieved that, for a moment, I was able to breathe.

My phone blinked in the dark, and I reached for the screen. It was Katsia, providing me with the details. There were only two of them, Raman and his friend Bahdan, both shot up. Raman died. Bahdan got paralyzed, and only after a while could he call an ambulance. At the moment, Bahdan was in intensive care. Mikola, Raman's closest friend, was out of it on sleeping pills. That was all the news.

My mind immediately fixated on Bahdan. I couldn't shake the memory of his shifty eyes and sly grin from the last time I saw him backstage at Raman's concert. Bahdan's skinny torso wrapped in a coral sweater as he dashed around with a camera, brazenly asking girls to let him touch their boobs. The image of his smug smile lingered in my mind like a stain. And now, he let Raman die and somehow managed to survive himself. He probably didn't even try to stop Raman from doing drugs. What a wimp. Disgust churned in my stomach as I swallowed back the rising nausea.

Then, my thoughts turned to Mikola, and my heart plummeted. The mental image of him, a towering figure now reduced to a helpless, slumbering state on his couch, was tearing my heart apart. The once boisterous, humorous, and self-assured goofball had turned into a little boy, with fear in his big blue eyes and tousled wheat-colored hair, wronged by the world.

I didn't remember how I fell asleep that night. Everything was a blur. The only thing I remembered was how I was lying in bed, thinking that I already had those thoughts before. Thoughts about the grim prospect of failing to save him. What would happen if he died? I tried so hard to push those thoughts away, believing that thoughts do materialize. Yet, despite my efforts, I couldn't help but imagine a world without him. It felt like my entire life was dying out along with Raman. Those thoughts brought me severe anxiety, prompting me to rush to my phone to check if Raman was online. And now... the very thing I had dreaded had come to pass. What had I been afraid of? What was the point of getting nervous?

CHAPTER 6

January 2014–March 2014

It was the 17th of January. Three days had slipped by since my birthday, and there we were, on a bustling Friday night at the dimly lit and packed Hooligan bar. The music hadn't yet reached its full volume, and the compact, tall room buzzed with the rumble of chatter.

I sank into the soft leather couch, enjoying the respite from socializing. Leaning gently against Natasha's shoulder, I rested my head upon it. I suddenly felt the urge to curl up by her side and just lay there, whisper-talking all night.

I glanced at the bag nestled in the corner of the adjacent sofa. A gift from Natasha was inside. I smiled at the thought. The warmth of her shoulder made me feel at ease.

Raising my eyes to the crowd, I spotted a familiar face in the distance. There he was, at the very end of the crowd, next to the tall industrial windows. Everything around him was immersed in darkness, but his face was highlighted by a radiant yellow light. He laughed, engaged in a conversation with the people around him.

"Natasha," I said, raising my head and leaning in closer to her ear. "is that Raman UFO?"

She had already been looking in that direction. "Yes, it's him."

She smiled, and we both continued gazing at him in awe. How is that possible that we ended up in the same place? This is fucking destiny.

I didn't want to drink. I didn't want to dance. I simply wished to freeze time right there.

I stared at Raman, hoping he would suddenly look at me, notice me, and smile back. But, within a heartbeat, he disappeared. I kept scanning the crowd, searching for his face among others, but he was gone.

"Hello!" Natasha's buoyant voice pierced my bubble, and I turned to see who she was talking to.

Before I could get a clear view, Natasha stood up, obscuring my line of sight. The loud music drowned out their voices, leaving me to watch as she extended her arms to wrap the man's shoulders in an embrace. His pale arms encircled her waist, and then I saw his face above her shoulder. It was *his* face. Natasha was wrapped in Raman's arms right before my eyes while I stood there, unsure of what to do.

They finally let go of each other and started talking, taking turns leaning into each other's ears, shouting over the music. I waited patiently for Natasha to introduce me, but she didn't seem to notice me standing behind her.

After a brief moment, they hugged again. Raman waved a quick goodbye and walked away. Natasha turned to me with a smile and sat back down on the couch.

What the fuck? I couldn't believe she didn't bother introducing me to him.

"So funny! What a coincidence," she finally said, staring into her phone. "Do you want to get another drink?"

"No, I'm good."

I sat back on the couch, grabbed the glass of whiskey from the coffee table, and took a hefty swig. Placing the glass back with a thump, I stood up. I had no mood to keep partying. I just wished I could go home. I headed to the bathroom, leaving Natasha alone.

The wait in line seemed interminable, and even my shoulders began to tense from standing for so long. Finally, the door swung open, and Raman stumbled out, laughing hysterically. He teetered, clutching the wall for support, before bursting into laughter once more. A tall, skinny girl followed behind him, giggling and casting her eyes downward in embarrassment. I took two steps forward and locked the door behind me, trying to calm my racing heart. Breathe. The bright red walls of the bathroom, covered in countless tiny stickers and writings, made me nauseous.

I lowered the toilet lid and sat down. I stared at the door in front of me, unable to think. They fucked. Right here, right in this bathroom stall. How can I be so stupid? He doesn't even remember me. I'm nothing. I'm really nothing to him. The tears welled up in my eyes.

"Calm down," I whispered to myself as I quickly wiped away the tears and cleaned my nose with toilet paper. From my pocket, I took out a small mirror to make sure there were no signs of crying on my face. I flushed the toilet, took a deep breath, and left the restroom. Heading straight for the bar, I ordered another glass of whiskey. I got back to the couch and killed the glass in one sip.

I didn't see Raman anymore that night. The alcohol helped me erase his face from my mind, at least for the night.

O

The incident at Hooligan slipped from my thoughts until I saw Raman in a dream. I woke up early, the room still shrouded in darkness and silence. Only a faint, feeble blue light filtered through the crack between the curtain and the wall.

Stretching my body, I retreated back under the comfort of the blanket, shivering. I gazed at the ceiling, a smile slowly spreading across my face.

I replayed the dream in my mind and immediately felt like my body had started filling up with warmth. I reminisced about Raman's face and the way he talked to me.

In the dream, we were close friends, and his smiling face, his laughter, his words, all of it felt so genuine and comforting. It was just a conversation, but it left me with a profound sense of closeness to him.

I thought about Raman's face in front of mine, and a wave of goosebumps danced along my arms. Jesus, it felt so good.

O

A few days later, I found myself in my room, getting dressed for a concert. The darkness outside had already settled in, and the idea of ditching the show and staying home instead was tempting. Yet, a part of me was determined to go, to prove to everyone, and perhaps to myself, that I could do it on my own. *No one wanted to join? Whatever!* Although, the prospect of going alone didn't really excite me that day. Even my dad wouldn't be at the venue. I sighed.

I arrived at the club just when the concert was about to start and made my way straight to the dance floor, aiming to blend in and not look like I had come alone. I stood close to the stage, and within minutes, the space behind me was almost entirely occupied. The anticipation in the air was palpable, with people impatiently screaming for the band to come out.

Standing next to me was a guy slightly taller than me and a pretty short girl. Out of nowhere, two tall, fancy chicks appeared and stood in front of the couple. The shorter girl awkwardly stared right at the taller girl's shoulder blades. She then glanced up at the guy beside her and shrugged.

The guy gradually shifted his attention to the intruders and spoke up. "We are actually standing here."

One of the girls turned around, flapping her long hair over the shorter girl's face, and arched an eyebrow at him.

"I'm sorry, what exactly are you trying to say here?" She didn't even look at his companion and responded with condescending disdain. "If I feel like it, I can make you disappear from here in a second." She spat the words at him and returned her gaze to the stage.

The guy wasn't about to back down. "Can't you see she's shorter than you? She can't see anything!"

"Listen, boy," she retorted without turning toward him. "What do you want from us!?" Then, abruptly pivoting, she extended a long, slender finger adorned with acrylic nails, pointing it at his face. "Are you fucking mental?"

I looked at the surrounding people, witnessing a mixture of shock and disbelief on their faces. Everyone had temporarily forgotten about the stage as they watched this unfolding drama.

But as soon as the smoke filled the stage, and the performance began, the incident faded into the background, and I, too, felt at peace again. However, it wasn't the end.

Just when I thought I had managed to push it all to the back of my mind and immerse myself in the music, someone jabbed me in the ribs. At first, I didn't even realize it was an accidental prod from someone's bony elbow. I winced in pain and instinctively looked up to see who it was from. The girl whose elbow I felt in my ribs didn't even notice me and continued her wild dance. Right behind her, those same troublesome girls from earlier came into view, and it became apparent that they were all part of the same group. These people were utterly unhinged, flailing their limbs and thrashing their heads around like complete lunatics. I thought this nightmare would never end.

I tried to focus on the show and not pay attention to them, but it was impossible. Another person joined their group, and I caught a glimpse, out of the corner of my eye, that it was a guy. I turned my head and there he was, Raman, standing right in front of me, mere inches away. For a moment, the time had stopped. I couldn't move. Until I realized he had come there with one of the girls. They held hands and hugged each other. He kissed her.

Suddenly, the story took an abrupt turn. These four started moving in a dance, although describing it as dancing would be a generous stretch—they were more like writhing, convulsing, and jumping in a fit of madness. These guys weren't drunk. There was something more than that. Back then, I didn't know quite well what it meant to be high, but it was apparent that something bizarre was happening in front of me. And it scared me. A deep anxiety churned in my stomach, warning me that if they noticed my presence, they might do something bad. They could hurt me. Raman could hurt me.

Furthermore, the situation kept escalating. Raman, his girlfriend, and one of her friends started dancing together. Then Raman pulled his girlfriend's friend even closer and kissed her. His arms wrapped around her waist as his girlfriend turned around and left the scene. I wasn't sure if Raman noticed that because he kept dancing with her friend, kissing her neck and grabbing her thighs.

The girl who had initially caught my attention wore a disapproving expression that mirrored my own growing sense of discomfort. She stretched her arms between the two and pushed them aside.

"Stop making out with a man who isn't yours! What the fuck do you think you're doing?"

The other one just looked back at her, and the three of them burst into laughter.

Later on, the girl, whom I presumed to be his girlfriend, came back. She stretched up on her tiptoes to whisper something into Raman's ear.

He responded with a hearty laugh, wrapping her in his arms. "Come on, everything's fine!"

As the night wore on, all four of them continued with the same shit. I was disgusted. I hated him. He disappointed me. I saw more and more evidence of what an asshole he was, but I couldn't help but wish to be closer to him, in all senses. His proximity was driving me crazy.

I couldn't bear to stay there any longer, so I dashed outside. My stomach churned, and I threw up right by the club's entrance.

As I straightened up, I realized I was carefully observed by a bunch of people standing by the doors. Hastily, I wiped my mouth and bolted away into the darkness, my only thought was to get back home.

Home. I needed to go home.

CHAPTER 7

August 2017

"Ignat totally called it about Raman dying in August." Mentioning the predictions of the psychic I talked to recently was the only condolence Natasha offered following Raman's death. She didn't seem to give a shit about it. All she seemed to care about was that Ignat was right. So what? How could she think of something like that?

The following day, I found myself on a bus headed to Mahilyow. The bus was filled with people, all sitting in awkward silence. It was still early, but the morning sun cast a sweltering heat upon us. The stifling air filled my nostrils, making me nauseous just thinking about it. I put on my sunglasses, hiding the narrow streaks of tears running down my cheeks.

The next two hours were a blur. No thoughts, no feelings, just silent tears cascading down my face, creating narrow rivulets that trailed down my neck and vanished beneath the neckline of my black jersey dress.

Upon arriving at Mahilyow, I made my way straight to Natasha's office, nestled within a shopping mall. As I entered, the crisp, cool air embraced me, sending shivers down my arms.

I entered Natasha's room, feeling all the anger and despair. But when I saw her, exhaustion washed over me, and I broke into tears.

"Aw, come here, my girl," she stood up and spread her arms.

I approached, wrapping my arms around her, burying my face in her shoulder as I sobbed heavily.

When my sobs subsided, Natasha leaned back and cupped my face in her hands. Her eyes bore into mine as she uttered, "It was his choice."

Confused, I shook my head and took a step back. Her face bore an unsettling mix of calmness and something else, something I couldn't read through immediately, something like... indifference. Yes, her face showed no sign of care or worry. Her face was cold.

"Will you guys come to the funeral?" I asked, desperate to change the subject. Given how hard Natasha and Pasha had worked to stay out of anything related to Raman, I assumed they wouldn't be there. But I was wrong.

"Of course."

O

For the rest of the day, I quietly sat there, watching Natasha finish her work. When she finally wrapped up, we walked home. Neither of us felt the need to take a cab. The freshness of the evening air promised some sort of temporary relief, so we leisurely made our way along Piershamajskaja Street, then Chaliuskincau Street, until we arrived back at her home.

The rest of the evening was enveloped in silence. Only by the night, when Pasha came home, carrying with him the faint scent of alcohol and cigarettes, did the atmosphere become calmer, and the tension gradually eased.

We just sat there in the living room, quietly talking and reminiscing about how it all started. The room was lit by the Christmas lights left on the wall for several months. Through the condensation on the balcony windows, I could see the beaming traffic lights. I felt at home. For a minute, I made peace with the fact that he was gone. I could finally breathe again.

As Natasha got up to head to the bathroom, Pasha leaned closer to me and whispered, "He had a girlfriend there, in Saint Petersburg. Nina. She's bringing him here together with his parents. Just thought you should know." He swiftly shifted the topic when Natasha appeared in the doorway. "So, I think I'll go pick Siargei and Katsia up early tomorrow and bring them here."

"Yes, good idea," Natasha answered. "We have to be at the graveyard by 2 p.m." She bent down to caress the cat playing around her feet.

The news about Raman's girlfriend didn't particularly upset me. I knew something was going on in his life, but I was still curious. I grabbed my phone and opened Instagram. Through his page, I quickly found her profile and started scrolling through the pictures, wondering what exactly he liked about her.

Nina looked young, likely in her early twenties. Her short blonde hair framed an open and innocent face, her blue eyes sparkled with a playful charm. She was definitely cute, but he wasn't the kind of guy who would date someone for just being cute. He could get anyone but chose her.

I set the phone aside and looked at the sky beyond the window. The initial calmness I had felt was soon overtaken by nervousness about meeting Katsia. I didn't understand what she must have been feeling after everything that had happened. I had no idea how to approach her, and in truth, I wasn't sure what to expect from tomorrow. It felt like this day and all my future existence was slipping into an abyss, leaving nothing behind.

Nothing at all.

CHAPTER 8

April 2015

After a month of radio silence, Natasha's message broke the stillness.

> \>
>
> *Giiiirl, you gotta come to Mahilyow next weekend!*
>
> *YOU HAVE TO!!!*

Weirdly enough, it brought a smile to my face. I didn't understand Natasha's approach to friendships and her inconsistent presence in my life, but for some reason, my resentment toward her was completely gone. Instead, a sense of anticipation began to stir within me, despite not even knowing what she meant by her message.

My contemplation was interrupted by the abrupt slam of the office door, as the accountant hurried past me, clutching a stack of papers. Ira, whose desk sat directly across from mine, and I exchanged fleeting glances before quickly returning our gazes to the computer screens.

The text on my monitor was completely blurry while my mind wandered around Natasha's message. What could it be about? Another party? A concert, perhaps? Maybe even a KOMA concert? Natasha knew how crazy in love I was with them.

Unable to contain my curiosity any longer, I snatched my phone. I was right. It was KOMA's concert. I couldn't help but smile, imagining a trip to Mahilyow for their gig. However, the reason Natasha desperately wanted my company at the concert was not KOMA. It was John Doe, the supporting band. Although I didn't know much about the band, I was aware that Mikola, Pasha's closest friend, was its leader. Hanging out with Mikola promised lots of fun, and I was all in.

It wasn't until later that I recalled Raman used to be a part of John Doe. The more I thought about it, the more nervous I became. I couldn't determine whether it was excitement or anxiety bubbling within me, but my body surely felt it—something big was on the horizon.

Without further ado, I called the bus company and secured the next available ticket to Mahilyow. I wanted to get there as soon as possible, as I couldn't be alone anymore. The prospect of seeing Raman was driving me to the brink of insanity. I wanted it so badly but was too scared to even dream about it. What if I didn't see him at all or only saw him on the stage? The latter was actually the likelier outcome. Or maybe I was just afraid that my dreams could come true and wasn't ready for that.

"Janina, stop!" I said out loud to myself to quell my anxiety. I then hastily threw some clothes into the suitcase and rushed to the bus station.

O

The bus felt unseasonably chilly for early April, with condensation on the windows that gave it a wintry vibe. The almost empty bus offered little distraction from the continuous playback of scenarios in my head. Will he be there? What will happen tomorrow night? One thing was certain—something would happen, and I had no doubts about it.

I got off the bus next to the diner "Buffet." I tugged open the weighty door, immediately embraced by the warmth inside. I looked back down at the suitcase, trying to drag it over the doorstep. I was scared to raise my eyes, as I knew I could run into anyone there. And I wasn't ready for that.

I glanced briefly at the menu above the barista's head and ordered three iced coffees. After settling my wallet back into my bag, I scanned the surroundings—only two families with children. I exhaled a sigh of relief.

It was warm and quiet inside. The curtains swayed gently in the breeze from an open window. The entrance door swung open, and the curtain billowed up before gently falling back into place. I held my breath for a moment and turned my head toward the noise. A man entered and joined one of the families. Phew.

"Three coffees for Janina!" the barista called out.

I grabbed the cardboard holder with the coffee cups, exchanged a smile with the barista, and left.

Excitement bubbled in my throat. My anxiety had dissolved. Everything around me felt like a good sign. Every detail held significance.

Arriving at Natasha's building, I buzzed the intercom, and she promptly unlocked the door. I ascended the stairs, the scent of dampness in the stairwell evoking fond childhood memories. For some reason, I always loved this smell.

I opened the apartment door, and the cat snuck out. Natasha, wearing a bathrobe and a towel on her head, ran after the rascal. I laughed and muttered an apology before stepping inside. Pasha came out of the kitchen and hugged me.

"I'm making vegan shawarmas!"

"Niiiiice! Could you also grab the coffees?"

I handed him the drinks and kicked off my shoes. Soon after, Natasha returned with the cat in her arms, and she enveloped me in a hug.

"Baby, I'm so happy you're finally here."

"Me too."

Once we'd finished eating, Pasha got ready for work. As soon as the door closed behind him, I asked Natasha the gnawing question, "Is Raman still in the band?"

"Who?" Natasha stopped washing dishes for a second and glanced back at me. "Ah, him... I don't know, Janina," she replied and returned to her task.

I picked up the remote and switched on the TV, sensing anxiety growing in my stomach like a slowly unwinding thread. The cozy plaid I sat on felt soft, and the cat leaped onto the couch to join me.

When Natasha had finished with the dishes, she crawled onto the couch, nestling beside me. She rested her head on my shoulder, and we stayed for the next couple of hours in complete silence.

I awoke as the room grew dim, feeling a cool breeze from the window against my skin. The TV had shut off, leaving the room awash in a soothing blue hue. I carefully slid my shoulder from beneath Natasha's head and gently placed a pillow in its stead.

I tiptoed to the bathroom and closed the door with a hushed click. Seated on the carpet, I opened Raman's Facebook profile.

He was online. Should I ask him about the concert? No, it would be weird. I then checked his Twitter, but there were no recent posts.

Jesus, why am I so worried about it? Attempting to rationalize away the anxiety provided little help. I had an inkling that something was about to happen.

I flushed the toilet, splashed my face with water, and went back to the room. Natasha was still in the same spot. I covered her with a blanket before heading to bed, still wrestling with the unanswered questions.

○

The following day, we all slept late. I didn't even notice how Pasha came home from work at the bar. I woke up from the sunlight flashing straight into my face and noticed that Natasha was already on her phone.

"Good morning," I mumbled, squinting against the brightness.

"Morning," Natasha replied, setting her phone aside and offering me a smile. "How did you sleep?"

"Surprisingly well!" I chuckled, thinking how tired I must have been last night to pass out so quickly. Even the pre-concert nerves didn't keep me awake.

In the early afternoon, Pasha left for the club to prepare everything for the show. We had agreed that Natasha and I would arrive a couple of hours before the concert. Once it was just Natasha and me again, I mustered the courage to discuss Raman.

"I feel so nervous."

"Why?" Natasha asked.

"I have this strange feeling about Raman," I began, sitting up on the mattress. "I mean, I really hope he'll be there tonight. I really want to see him, but it scares the shit out of me. I don't know why."

"Baby, you might be overthinking things. Even if he's there tonight, what can happen? Pasha and Mikola will be busy working, so it'll likely be just the two of us hanging out. Nothing bad can happen."

"I don't mean bad…" I trailed off.

"Then what is it?" Natasha pressed.

I opened my mouth and only sighed in response.

I lay back on the mattress. Natasha couldn't even notice that I wished he was there. I wanted so badly to meet him.

I didn't know what to say any longer, so I got up and started getting ready. Natasha switched on the music and joined me.

O

We were running out of time, so we took a cab to the venue. We entered Cuba, bypassing the lengthy line in just a few minutes. Inside the club, while standing in a hallway flanked by three imposing mirrors, it suddenly struck me that he was there. I just knew it. At that moment, I harbored no doubts.

The golden frames of the mirrors gleamed in the club's lighting, creating a surreal atmosphere. Sounds of instruments being tuned emanated from the stage. Natasha caught up with me and took hold of my hand, guiding me forward to the second floor and crossing the dance floor. I sank inside, afraid of looking at the stage, afraid of raising my eyes when someone was walking toward us. I was a bundle of nerves—anxious and shaking. Even though I desperately wanted to meet Raman, I wasn't ready to talk to him.

Natasha led me to the chill-out room, where Mikola was tending the bar. Quick handshake, a smile that looked more like a grimace on Mikola's face. He was friendly and nice, but I couldn't focus on anything he was saying. I needed to get drunk.

I walked alone to Pasha's bar located on the same floor, trying to get there without running into Raman. Pasha poured whiskey into two glasses and handed one to me.

"You're ok?"

"Yeah, just a bit nervous," I replied.

He smiled and moved away to attend to other clients, all while casually sipping his drink. I stared at my trembling hands gripping the glass.

"There you are!" I glanced up and saw Natasha standing beside me. She waved at Pasha, signaling for another drink, and then turned her surprised gaze to me. "I didn't realize you left. Everything's okay?"

"Yeah, of course!" I tried to force a smile. "I just wanted a drink before the show starts."

Natasha wandered to the balcony's edge to observe the activity downstairs. "Quite busy over there!"

I smiled at her, my gaze dropping to my glass. The distant thrum of a bass guitar seeped into the room, accompanied by the sound of the screaming crowd. It snapped me back to reality.

"Natasha, they're starting the show! Let's go downstairs!" I tugged her arm, urging her toward the dance floor. I looked back at her and saw the resisting smile on her face.

"I don't really want to stand in the crowd…" We paused for a moment.

"Where do you want to stand, then?" She started pissing me off. Didn't she see how excited I was, hoping he might perform tonight, longing to get closer to the stage?

She moved ahead of me, scanning the area for any available space around the dance floor. As we descended the stairs amidst the throngs of people, I realized every nook and cranny was occupied. Natasha squeezed between people standing in the stairwell and pulled me in to stand alongside her. I looked at her and smiled. It wasn't the worst spot, after all.

The stage lights flickered to life, and I saw him. Raman *was* in the band. For a moment, I forgot how to breathe, my grip tightening on the railing. I stood there in a stupor, unable to believe my eyes. It was him—my childhood crush, standing on the stage right before me. But he was no longer the cute teenager I remembered. I saw an insanely handsome man in front of me.

Jesus, he looked incredible. I couldn't stop looking at his tattoo. His entire left arm was inked in black, transitioning into fiery red and intricate designs near the elbow. I'd never seen anything as beautiful in my life. The most breathtaking part was where the tattoo ended, marked by a sharp line at his wrist, making his already beautiful, slender arm look exquisite. I couldn't hear the music, and I wasn't thinking about the band. I was just looking at Raman. His arms, shoulders, face, the shaved sides of his head, his hair, and the familiar birthmarks. It was him. I couldn't believe it.

Throughout the show, I struggled to breathe normally. I couldn't make sense of what was happening to me.

When the band left the stage, I still stood there, lost in my thoughts, attempting to comprehend the reality of the moment. Someone tapped my shoulder, and I turned around. Natasha motioned for me to follow her. In a quiet corner, she leaned in close and whispered in my ear, "If Pasha manages to bounce from work, we're heading to Raman's."

"To Raman's? Raman wh-h-h-ho?"

"Raman UFO."

I stepped back to see her face. She couldn't be joking. She smiled back at me. It must be true then. Is it really happening? I couldn't wrap my head around it. I wasn't nervous, no; I was certain we would make it there. I had no doubt this would be the night I'd met the famous Mr. Krasouski.

Only after I found out that Pasha managed to leave early, which meant that we were actually going to Raman's, I started to panic. Did I look ok? What am I going to do there? What am I going to say? This stupid crazy anxiety.

I started pissing the guys off by asking tons of questions. They explained we were heading to a place where Raman lived, but no one had any clear idea of who would be there or what we would be doing. The only thing I knew for certain was that we were going home to get ready, pick up Mikola and his girlfriend, buy some food and drinks, and then set off for Raman's.

I swallowed.

O

On the way home from Cuba, we found ourselves in a cab, Natasha and I occupying the back seat, Pasha sitting in the front. I looked out of the window and thought that at least I could go home and change. Not sure why it made me feel calmer—I didn't have many clothes with me—but it gave me some relief.

We barged into the apartment. Natasha headed for the bathroom to touch up her makeup. I rushed to my bags in a frantic search for something to wear, and Pasha strolled over to the kitchen to pour a glass of wine.

"Want some?" he offered.

"No! I have no time!" I shot him an impatient look and continued digging through the pile of clothes. "What should I wear?"

"You girls are funny!" Pasha grinned.

The bathroom door swung open, and Natasha walked to me. She crouched down and closed her eyes. "Is the eyeliner okay?"

"Yes, it's good!"

She got up and went back to the bathroom. Passing by Pasha, she gave him a quick kiss and walked away.

I finally decided what to wear. Instead of one gray shirt, I put on another one, together with a black sweatshirt, black jeans, and ugly brown Chelsea boots. It was a mess, but it would have to do.

We hailed another cab and headed to pick up Mikola and his girlfriend Alesia. All together, we went to a store and bought a hell ton of food and alcohol.

After passing by countless gray high-rise residential buildings, we reached the destination. The car door slammed, and within seconds, we stood in complete darkness. I could hear faint voices and giggles in the distance, but nothing was visible. I felt a pang of anxiety, exacerbated by the squeaky laughter of girls in the vicinity.

Taking a deep breath to steady myself, we followed the sounds, unsure of the path ahead. Mikola took out his phone to light up the road. Suddenly, the path ended, revealing a steep descent of stairs. At the bottom, a bonfire and a crowd of people came into view, making my stomach churn. But there was no turning back now; we had to continue.

When we came to the fire, no one even looked at us. Mikola made raucous noise, unpacking our supplies, and regaling humorous stories in an attempt to capture the crowd's attention. I looked at him and couldn't help but think he was a bit of a goofball but undeniably entertaining.

"Raman," a bold and assertive voice cut through the chatter, prompting me to turn my head.

There stood Raman, extending his long, slender arm toward me. I looked up into his face, where little fires danced in his dark eyes, reflecting the flickering bonfire. He narrowed his eyes and offered a warm smile, expecting a handshake.

"Janina," I responded, my voice surprisingly steady.

I had no idea how I managed to control the internal chaos. I stood right in front of him. He was looking at me. He was holding my hand. It was insane.

He returned my smile, released my hand, and rejoined the conversation with others. I deflated. Clearly, he didn't have much interest in continuing to talk with me.

I stayed in the same spot, observing the scene around me. It was mainly a gathering of guys, with just a couple of girls. People were scattered in small groups around the bonfire. I glanced upward, trying to take in the surrounding landscape, noticing that the location was enclosed by high hills.

The house stood close to the staircase we had descended. It was a big house, but not completely finished. Plain walls, building materials scattered around. For some reason, I had imagined a more luxurious setting, befitting Raman himself.

A loud laugh grabbed my attention. Raman joined in the laughter and added, "Chicks' pussies taste like beer!" The group erupted into more laughter.

Playfully, I said, "So you're sticking to beer tonight? No other options?"

Raman chuckled, gazing at me with amusement, and I felt a sense of pride for my witty remark.

"Hey, Raman, could you make a hole for me?" one of the girls purred in a flirtatious tone, handing him a bag of chips.

Raman shot her a condescending look, opened the bag, and handed it back. He didn't react to her flirt at all. That's when I realized all the girls at the party were acting the same way— trying hard to flirt with him and capture his attention. Didn't they understand how desperate it made them look? I couldn't help but wonder why they needed to humiliate themselves like that.

What I further noticed was that it wasn't just the girls vying for Raman's attention—the guys were doing the same. They all shadowed Raman's every move, seeking his approval. They echoed his words and laughed at his jokes. Each one tried to outdo the other in winning Raman's favor. But Raman kept looking at me. All the while, I caught his eyes on me, but it wasn't the same sinister look. It was something different. Curiosity. Exploring.

I settled on a bench and fished out a chocolate bar from my pocket, savoring the first bite. Just then, Raman took a seat beside me.

"Janina? A strange question, but are you Miazhevich, by any chance?"

"Uhm… Yes, Miazhevich," I replied, trying to conceal my shock. Out of the corner of my eye, I noticed the girls fell silent, watching.

"What did he say?" they whispered among themselves. "Who is she?"

Raman glanced at them and responded with pronounced eloquence, "Whaaat? You don't know who Janina Miazhevich is?" He laughed, then turned his attention back to me.

"How do you know me?" I asked in surprise.

"Well, from the past..." he replied with a teasing smile, his eyes locked onto mine.

"How? Tell me!" I nudged him to get him to share.

"Do you know the band the Rockets?"

"I knew it!" I burst into laughter, momentarily forgetting the presence of others. At that moment, nothing else mattered. "I remember you! But how do you know me?" I was still bewildered by the fact that a guy from my favorite band knew my name.

"I just do," he said, scratching the back of his head as he gazed into the fire. He seemed lost in his memories, while I cherished every second of looking at his handsome face in the orange glow of the flames. "I remember your dad. Remember how he used to talk about you."

"Oh, Jeez... I can only imagine what kind of stories he shared." I blushed, recalling how my dad always embarrassed me by recounting awkward anecdotes about me to musicians.

"No, no, it was cute!" He waved his arms in denial. "He was telling good things about you."

I was looking at his face right next to mine and couldn't take my eyes off it. Tiny birthmarks were scattered around his face. When he smiled, a little dimple appeared on the right side of his chin. I was thinking about how I would run my hand through his hair when he looked at me in question and said, "Janina?"

It snapped me back to reality. "Huh?"

"You're eating plain bread," he observed and rose, strolling over to the group near the fire. "I'll take it, ok?" Without waiting for an answer, Raman plucked a freshly grilled sausage from the guy's hands and brought it to me. "Take the sausage. Bread is better with a sausage."

I extended the piece of bread, and he placed the sausage on it. Once more, Raman's eyes met mine, and he smiled.

Raman pulled a beer can from somewhere beneath the bench, popping it open with a soft hiss. As he raised it to his lips, I noticed two rings on his pinky and ring finger.

"What are those?" I titled my head, squinting to read the letters on the rings.

"Death plays," Raman replied, setting the beer down beside his foot. With a subtle movement, he adjusted the rings to make the words visible to me.

And there we were, sitting side by side, me and the guy I'd been in love with for the past nine years, chatting about life. Other people ceased to exist. All I knew was Raman. He shared jokes, asked about me, trying to get to know me. It all felt surreal but at the same time, so normal.

Raman's phone rang. He checked the screen, got up without answering, and said, "I'll be right back," as he glanced down at me.

I smiled in response and looked away. I sat alone, watching as the enchantment of talking with Raman gradually faded. I returned to reality.

Natasha and Pasha were busy talking with someone. Above that, I suddenly felt too tired to stand up and walk toward them. So I remained where I was, gazing at the fire and finishing my sausage.

"Hey, lonely girl!" A dark-haired guy holding a can of beer sat down beside me, extending his hand. "Andrei."

I shook his hand without even looking at him, my gaze fixated on Raman ascending the stairs I had taken a while ago.

Andrei seemed to seek some company, as he was prone to talk to me. His monotone voice was lulling me to sleep. I nodded in response to whatever he was saying, preoccupied with thoughts of the past few hours spent with Raman.

Suddenly, I noticed two figures descending the stairs—Raman and a girl. She was a slender girl with a doll-like face, her long hair bouncing with each step down the stairs. I swallowed hard, feeling my self-esteem plummet.

They approached the bonfire, standing on the opposite side of me, opposite to where Raman and I had been just moments ago. He paid no more attention to me and fixed his gaze entirely on her.

Surprisingly, what caught my attention was the way he spoke to her. His words dripped with sarcasm, each one delivered with an air of condescension as if he viewed her as the most insignificant and intellectually challenged person on Earth. Yet, she didn't seem fazed and continued to laugh at his jokes.

I reached for my phone and sent a text to Ian, my crazy love from a year ago—a married man, much older than me, with whom I had spent a year, sharing him with his wife and another continent across the ocean. Yet, all those feelings had somehow dissipated into thin air the moment I met Raman.

<

I guess unavailable guys are my destiny

>

Got it

They probably are your destiny haha

I let out a sigh and glanced back at Raman. How had it felt so incredibly real just moments ago, and now he was engrossed in conversation with this pretty woman? Was it his girlfriend?
The screen lit up with another message from Ian.

>

So who is he??

<

A dude from the Rockets

The one I had a crush on when I was a teen

His girlfriend is standing right next to him and he surely wants something from me

I don't understand what the fuck is going on

And also, he knows me

I'm shocked

>

Well, cool

I wasn't sorry. I was hurting, and I desperately needed to hurt someone else. Someone who was madly in love with me but couldn't do shit to turn things around for me. *Fucking cowards, these men.*

I locked the phone and looked in front of me. After the screen's light no longer blinded me, I could still see Raman standing there. It had indeed happened. I was falling more and more in love with him, but I struggled to admit it, even to myself.

His skin had taken on a warm, yellowish hue from the fire's glow. He held a beer, his elbows bent. He was looking at the fire, not noticing me staring at him. He was so insanely beautiful. His long fingers, the black tattoo peeking from under his sleeve. He glanced down, absently prodding something with his foot, his face devoid of any hint of a smile.

A drop landed on my cheek, and I instinctively looked up, wondering if it was the start of rain, but a big wet chunk fell on my nose. Snow! At the end of April! Enormous snowflakes fell on us and the bonfire. People started moving, unsure how to react. We were laughing, making fun of it.

It took a few moments for us to realize the snowfall wouldn't cease, prompting a mad dash into the house to rescue any salvageable food.

We rushed inside, leaping onto the couches. Natasha sat in the corner. I occupied the seat next to her, leaving the third seat on the couch empty. That was where Raman should sit. Please, I want him to sit there! He was there with his girlfriend, and I was aware he might not be the right person to hang out with, but I wanted it so badly. I just wanted to hold on to the moment with him for as long as possible.

He entered the room and sat right by my side. Yes! His

girlfriend followed suit, taking the small space on the other side of him. Fuck.

Suddenly, Raman got up and left, and his girlfriend slid over to the space beside me on the couch. I looked at her and smiled, unsure of what to say.

She smiled back and asked, "So, are you from around here? What's your name?"

"No, I'm from Miensk. My name is Janina. Actually, it's my first time meeting most of these people."

She laughed, and I laughed too. For some reason, chatting with her made me feel more at ease.

"Sviataslava," she said, extending her hand. I gently shook it. "I live in Miensk too, but I'm from here."

"Yeah? What are you doing there?"

"Studying. And working. I'm a designer."

"Niiice. Whe…"

Raman squeezed back into the tiny space between the two of us and turned to me, handing me a banana. "Take it, sweetheart. You must be hungry."

I hesitantly accepted the banana, averting my gaze. *What. The. Fuck.*

Sviataslava didn't seem to react at all to her boyfriend acting like this with other girls. I was completely baffled by the situation.

I made an effort to breathe and stay calm, but a blush surged across my face. Raman's leg was warm, pressed right against mine. I glanced down and realized our legs were tightly entwined, sending a wave of excitement rippling through my stomach. He put his arm on his lap, and it slowly rolled into the pit between my leg and his. Through my jeans, I could feel the comforting heat of his arm. I looked at it again and couldn't get my eyes off it. The very arm I had been captivated by during the entire concert now lay on my lap. I couldn't believe my eyes. I wanted to take a picture, but I knew that in any case, this scene was imprinted on my memory.

Natasha lightly tapped my left knee. "I'll go out to have some air." I smiled at her as she left.

Raman's beers disappeared one bottle after another, and in a short while, for the first time, I saw someone whom my friends called afterward *normal* Mr. Krasouski. The one spilling out bullshit, disgusting dirty jokes, and tons of offenses to everyone around. He didn't say or take anything seriously. He looked at me with the same look in his eyes as before and asked, "Will you let me taste your beer pussy?"

I couldn't believe what I was seeing. With each passing moment, Raman sank further into degradation before my eyes. I felt anger rising within me—not just toward him, but toward myself for expecting anything more. For setting my hopes so high. It was becoming painfully clear: he was not for me.

Then, Raman got up and left. Sviataslava moved closer to me and uttered, "You are very beautiful and special."

"Huh? What do you mean?" Her comment caught me off-guard.

"Nothing, really. I just wanted to take a moment to remind you that you are special. Just so you know." She smiled again.

Just as I was about to answer her, Pasha suddenly appeared at my side, leaning in close to whisper in my ear, "Natasha isn't feeling well. We need to leave. Are you coming with us?"

My heart sank. No, no, no. Pleeeeease… I can't leave! I'm not ready for the night to end!

"Yeah, sure, let's go."

Sviataslava was busy texting with someone, so I rose from my seat and followed Pasha out into the hallway. As I reached the hallway, the bathroom door swung open, and Raman stumbled out, guffawing loudly.

"Ahh, baby, do you have condoms?" he slurred, leaning heavily on my shoulder, almost causing me to lose my balance. The stench of cheap alcohol and weed clung to him.

I dropped him off and said, "We have to go now."

"Alright," he hiccupped. "Bye."

Disgust, disappointment, and a sense of betrayal washed over me. Yet, it was my own self who had betrayed me. What had I expected from this? Did I truly believe Raman would change just because of me? That a bad boy would suddenly transform after meeting a good girl? Never.

O

When we finally arrived home, I didn't have any energy to continue thinking about what had happened. Natasha went straight to bed and passed out right after. I wandered into the kitchen, where Pasha uncorked a bottle of wine.

"Want some?" he offered.

"Yeah…" I replied, my voice barely above a whisper.

He pulled out an extra glass from the cupboard and poured a bit of wine into it. I took the glass and sat down on the floor. Pasha settled beside me, leaning against the cabinet.

I struggled to find the words to explain to him how I couldn't stop thinking about Raman. I needed to go back, but how…

"Would you go back? Now that Natasha is asleep?" I whispered.

"Nah… I can't. She'll never forgive me." He chuckled softly, his laughter belying the sadness in his eyes. I was sure that he wanted to go there as much as I wanted to see Raman.

Unsure of what else to say, I swirled the wine in my glass and let out a deep sigh.

"Janina, don't get too close to him. He won't bring you any good."

CHAPTER 9

August 2017

I cracked my eyes open, the room a dim and unfocused blur. The weight of my heavy eyelids won, and they descended, leaving me in disoriented darkness. Where am I?

Making another effort, I blinked and squinted, gradually discerning the surroundings. Mahilyow.

I turned my head. Natasha lay next to me. It wasn't a dream. Raman did die. The harsh reality pressed down on my chest, and I exhaled. What will happen now?

The ticking of the watch on my wrist filled the silence, along with the faint rustle of tires gliding over the asphalt outside. I imagined cars slowing down as they gently turned into the courtyard. How nice it must be outside right now. The tantalizing freshness of the shade under the lush tree branches. That saturated dark green color that only happens at the beginning of summer was somehow back once again.

A low, drawn-out sigh escaped my lungs. My tense shoulders slackened, and my hands moved to my face, covering my eyes.

I inhaled more rapidly, anxiety tightening its grip, thoughts whirling in a chaotic vortex. I wasn't ready for the day to start.

Amidst this internal storm, a hushed "How are you?" reached my ears, and I turned to Natasha.

She was looking at me, her eyes wide open, posing a question that didn't imply an answer. She was probably nervous to even say a word to me. Honestly, I wished she didn't say anything at all.

"I'm alright," I mumbled.

I climbed out of bed and headed to the bathroom, the cold floor jolting my senses. I took a few long strides, closed the door, and breathed a sigh of relief. Finally, I could be by myself.

I sat down on the carpet. Tears ran down my cheeks. I covered my mouth, trying to stay quiet. Raman... What should I do now? How should I talk to people? How is everyone managing?

The entrance door creaked, and voices filled the apartment. Katsia and Siargei had arrived, and Pasha had picked them up from the airport.

I took a deep breath, trying to calm myself down, and rose from my spot. I wiped my eyes with a quick hand motion to dry the tears.

I looked in the mirror. My face was a mess, red and swollen. Well, my friend died. How else could I look? I flushed the toilet and opened the door.

Katsia appeared in the hallway, holding a cardboard holder with four cups of coffee. In the darkness of the hallway, I could only discern the outline of her petite figure, skinny legs in dark leggings, and an oversized hoodie. Stepping into the light, her face lit up as she smiled at me. She wasn't wearing any make up, and her face was adorned only by a curtain of short, dark bangs. Eagerly, I took a step forward and wrapped her in a tight hug.

"How are you holding up?" she asked softly, touching my cheek.

"I'm okay. You know…" I replied with a shrug. "How are you?"

"Not surprised." Katsia giggled. "I've stopped being surprised by Mr. Krasouski giving me shit to handle."

Siargei laughed, hearing her remark, and I walked over to him to offer a hug.

"You good, Janina?"

"Yeah…"

"Miron doesn't reply to my messages," Katsia noted as she made her way to the kitchen. "I have no idea where we should be heading."

She left the paper coffee cups on the table and retreated to the balcony with her phone, trying to reach the second member of Raman's band, NPL, but with no success so far.

I plucked a coffee cup from the holder and sank onto the couch. The cat, familiar with my presence, leaped onto my lap, making herself comfortable.

"Aw, she adores you," Natasha remarked, snapping a quick picture with her phone. "She always does it when you come over."

Meanwhile, Pasha and Siargei occupied the floor, surrounded by the packaging from the coffee shop. Pasha unwrapped a sandwich while Siargei was chitchatting. Yet, Raman's name remained conspicuously absent from our discussion. It felt like we were all collectively avoiding the very reason that had brought us together.

"Miron, what the fuck!" Katsia finally managed to get through. "Where exactly is that? Can you send me the coordinates?"

Natasha walked to the balcony and slid the glass door shut. Even through the door, I could still hear Miron's voice on the other end. So weird. Just a couple of months ago, I'd been hanging out with him at Raman's place. I'd get high and listen to Miron's stardom-struck stories about his fangirls, wrinkling my nose in cringe and giggling at Raman's reaction. It seemed like yesterday.

As I listened intently to Katsia's call, the others started packing stuff to take off to the graveyard. It was time to leave. I slipped into a black dress and sneakers, brushed my teeth, and left the apartment.

We all piled into the car, with the girls in the back seat and the guys up front. Pasha hit play on the music player, and NPL's song filled the car. Do we really need to listen to that? It fucking hurts...

It felt like no one really cared. The phrase "Lived like a rock star and died like a rock star," spoken by one of the celebrities from the news, echoed in my thoughts.

Do you really think this is dope? Morons. I hate you all so much, fucking assholes... Does anyone understand that he died? Like, really died! It's not a fucking game...

CHAPTER 10

April 2015

I woke up before everyone else, as it usually happens when I'm in Mahilyow. I stretched my arms and turned my face toward the gentle morning sun that filtered through the curtains. A serene feeling washed over me, and I couldn't help but close my eyes and smile. It felt peaceful and quiet.

Suddenly, an unpleasant feeling started to tie a knot right above my stomach. Creeping anxiety from thinking that my last night's miracle was about to end. I didn't want to leave. God knew I didn't want to.

Thoughts of everything that had happened the night before occupied my mind. Raman... These thoughts were frightening me. I was scared. Scared to admit it might have been the last time I saw him, and that I'd never have the chance to talk to him like that again. I blamed myself for not staying longer, for missing an opportunity I might never have again.

I heard some rustling and turned my head to the bed. Natasha was tossing. The guys were about to wake up, which meant that I'd have to get going soon. But for now, I lay on my inflatable bed, scrolling through Raman's Instagram feed. I still couldn't believe I had met him just the day before. The image of his arm on my lap was imprinted in my mind. His tattoo. Damn, I hated myself for not coming back, for not spending more time with him. I should've done something.

I didn't want to follow him first on Instagram, but at the same time, I didn't know what else I could do. I was nervous he wouldn't react to it and wouldn't even notice that I started following him among all the other fangirls. So, I stared at his pictures, lost in contemplation.

Then I found him on Facebook and saw that he was online. It struck me that he might be holding his phone at that very moment, and anything I did would draw his attention. I had no options on my mind other than just liking a few of his pictures on Instagram. Aaaaand guess what? In that very instant, he followed me on Instagram and added me on Facebook. *Daaaaaamn. That was smooth!*

I couldn't contain my excitement, and I burst into laughter. Natasha turned her head to me with a look of surprise.

"Raman followed me on Instagram!" My voice bubbled with excitement, reminiscent of a child proudly showing a newly discovered treasure to their parents. I could feel myself shaking with joy.

"Wow." Natasha was indifferent, her face unchanging.

But I didn't care. Inside, I was flying high.

CHAPTER 11

August 2017

We stepped out of the car and surveyed the scene. The parking lot and driveway were densely packed with vehicles, and a sense of solemnity hung in the air. People dressed in black were hesitantly fumbling around.

Among the crowd, I spotted Miron and gestured toward him, catching Katsia's attention. She wordlessly made her way toward him, with Siargei following closely behind. Meanwhile, Pasha, Natasha, and I stood amidst the cars, unsure of what to do. I looked to the side, trying to avoid meeting eyes with Miron. Everything felt awkward.

Just then, another car arrived, and two girls and a guy came out of it. From a distance, I immediately recognized one of the girls, her blond hair, blue eyes, and gentle smile. Nina.

As the group approached us, she suddenly raised her eyes to me and softly uttered, "Hi."

"Hi," I replied.

A surge of bitterness welled up within me after looking at her. It wasn't even jealousy of the girl who managed to change him. It was pain, pain for her. She turned out to be just a kid. Her innocent face looked confused and lost. I realized that behind that Instagram image was just a little girl who had probably never dealt with death in her life. It wasn't as if the experience made dealing with it any easier, but she seemed totally unprepared. As if you can ever be prepared for something like this at all. I chuckled, thinking about that.

"Everyone, come on, let's go!" a loud male voice jarred me out of my thoughts.

People moved in the direction indicated by the voice, and I followed them. Amid the crowd, I spotted another familiar face moving toward us—Makar, Raman's friend and the leader of KOMA. Seeing a friendly face, I longed to run to him and get wrapped in his big arms. Instead, I said a dry "Hi," to which he respectfully nodded, shook Pasha's hand and continued on his way.

What a strange feeling. We all seemed to be friends when things were fun and easy, and now it felt awkward to show these people my vulnerability. I tried so hard to find any support in these faces, but everyone was hiding behind a mask of indifference.

As we continued walking, we arrived at an aged village house—a structure with peeling paint, a rickety roof, and tattered lace curtains on its windows. A sizable crowd had already gathered near the gate.

Natasha and I looked at each other in confusion, unsure of where to stand, what to do with the flowers we brought, and in general, what to expect.

I stood in silence, trying to figure it out, when I saw people swarming out of the entrance door. Next came the coffin. Men in dark clothes were carefully carrying it through the doorway.

Raman.

As they descended the stairs of the porch, they hoisted the coffin above their heads and balanced it on their shoulders. A brief pause allowed the assembled guests to pay their last respects before the procession made its way toward the graveyard, the guests following in silence.

I scampered, trying to keep up with the speed and be able to see Raman in the slightly tilted coffin. I looked at his face and couldn't take my eyes off it. It hurt so badly. It was him, his beautiful face. It just didn't settle in my mind that there was no life in it.

As I walked, I couldn't tear my eyes away from him. Out of the blue, it dawned on me that this was the last time I would ever see him. And I couldn't get enough of him. I desperately tried not to let a single second slip away.

Finally, we arrived at the road, where the men carrying the coffin placed it into the hearse. The car doors shut, and it drove away. I realized that Raman's body was being transported to the main entrance of the graveyard, while the guests were meant to take a shortcut through the forest. *Raman's body.* The thought echoed in my mind, distracting me from my own grief.

I watched Nina pass by, scurrying toward the head of the procession, and wondered once more about how she must have been feeling. Her skinny silhouette and sloped shoulders made me want to hug her. She was dressed in black, but her white slip-ons stood out. She wore no makeup and had the look of a child. Another girl approached her, and Nina responded with a smile, taking her by the elbow.

Natasha approached me, taking my hand. The warmth of her hand made me feel more at ease.

As we drew nearer, I noticed the crowd ahead had halted, a sea of mourners mingling with the tall pines. We came closer, but

I still couldn't see anything. Couldn't see Raman. *But wait, I need to see him!* I realized I desperately needed a chance to touch him and look him in the face the last time.

My attention returned to Nina, and I found myself wondering again what Raman had seen in her. She was cute, but nothing special, really. Her face was covered by the sunlight. She looked at Raman and gave him the biggest smile. So childish and helpless.

I noticed that Maksim, Raman's childhood friend, was also smiling. These people knew precisely what Raman would have wanted, and I knew it too, but I couldn't smile. Thank God, at least, I wasn't crying.

Then, I spotted Raman's parents in the crowd. His dad, with this good-hearted face, also smiling. But his mother appeared distant. I wondered what she was thinking about. She had lost her child. How hard it must have been to keep up a facade while dying inside.

As the eulogy began, a lump formed in my throat, and I immediately broke down. Tears streamed down my cheeks, and I realized I didn't even bring the napkins. I couldn't even wipe my fucking tears. I just stood there, in the middle of the forest, two meters away from the person I loved most, who was fucking *dead*. My sobbing intensified, my shoulders trembling with each convulsion.

Katsia gently touched my arm and handed me a napkin. I pressed it to my eyes and wept again. My breath came in heavy, uneven gasps, and I no longer heard the eulogy.

Katsia wrapped her arm around me, and I buried my face in her shoulder. She stroked my head and whispered comforting words in my ear, their meaning lost in the waves of my sorrow, but her voice was so soothing that I didn't dare to interrupt her.

After a while, I could breathe normally and wiped the smeared mascara off my face. I put the sunglasses on and scanned the surroundings. Mikola still didn't show up. Neither did Alesia, his girlfriend. Right behind me, I saw Sasha, crying all by herself. I remembered how I first met her, back then a 16-year-old girl, at Raman's place, where she would often emerge from his bedroom, draped only in a blanket, tiptoeing quietly toward the bathroom. Now, she was spewing tears around her beautiful face, sobbing. It looked like no one was going to comfort her. How come? The girl who knew everyone, who was always the center of attention, now stood alone, not needed by anyone. I wondered if I should come to her and offer her a napkin. But I didn't.

People began to approach the coffin one by one, leaving their flowers as a final farewell. I waited until the family and closest friends had their turn. Suddenly, the crowd stepped back; the coffin was sealed, and it was lowered into the ground.

Wait, I didn't get to say goodbye!

I glanced around, searching for answers, but found none. The coffin descended deeper and deeper, and that's when the realization hit me—it was over. My last opportunity to see him was slipping through my fingers.

I gazed up at the picture hanging on the cross, a photo of Raman from the beginning of his twenties. So young and handsome. So alive. And now… that was it. The coffin was under the ground. The cemetery workers were shoveling the grave.

I navigated my way through the crowd, determined to be near him. I knelt down and touched the ground, longing for a moment alone with him, away from the watchful eyes of the crowd. I wished the crowd behind me would disappear and stop watching me every second. I couldn't even bring myself to speak or whisper, as if the words were a secret I couldn't share.

I grabbed a handful of sand and threw it on the grave. "Bye," I said to Raman.

I placed my flowers on the pile by the grave and returned to Natasha and Pasha.

People around continued waiting in confusion, unsure of what to do next. Judging by their age, most of them probably weren't that familiar with funerals.

A long, mournful weeping caught my attention, and I turned to see an elderly lady beside me, tears streaming down her face. She was in anguish, lamenting, "It was his great-grandmother! She took him away from us! Why don't you listen to me?" Her sobs were interrupted by labored breathing, draining her strength, but she didn't seem to stop.

A woman in her thirties approached the old lady, cupped her face in her hands, and spoke softly and patiently as if consoling a little boy who'd just bruised his knee. Suddenly, they both burst into tears. I turned my head away. This was too painful to witness.

Then, a clearing of the throat drew my attention, and I saw Raman's father, holding a crumpled piece of paper, standing nervously. He ran a hand through his sparse, gray-streaked hair and began, "We'd like to invite you all to dinner." Pausing to gather his thoughts, he continued, "Nothing special. We just want to spend time with you, with people close to Raman. And we'll be happy to share this evening with you."

He smiled, but his voice wavered, and a surge of bitterness welled up within me. I exchanged a questioning glance with Natasha and Pasha.

"I don't think we should go there," Natasha frowned. "That would be weird. It seems more like a family gathering."

"Yeah, probably..." I agreed, torn between wanting to go and the fear of intruding. "But we do need to give his dad the money."

"How're you going to do that?" Pasha's voice trembled with anxiety. "We can't just come to him and give him the money."

"I'll talk to him anyway. I'll give him my money. We can either come all together, or I can give him your money as well."

Pasha handed me the rolled-up money, and I made my way to Zmicier. At that moment, I wasn't even nervous anymore. I felt ashamed, so awfully ashamed of myself, of the fact that I let it all happen. I haven't saved his son. I have done nothing. I felt guilty and ashamed.

Drawing near, I noticed Zmicier hugging the woman who earlier tried to comfort the old lady. It felt awkward to interrupt them, but he caught sight of me and let go of her.

"Hey… I'm very sorry," my voice broke. God, don't cry, don't cry. "Take it, please. Thank you."

"Thank *you*! Thank you for coming!" Zmicier responded with a warm, grateful smile. The entire world just disappeared when I looked into Raman's father's eyes and saw Raman there. "He loved you."

I held my breath for a moment, but then the dam broke. Tears flowed down my face, and I covered it with my hands, unable to stop crying. Zmicier pulled me closer and hugged me tightly, and I clung to him.

There we were, standing in the forest by his son's grave, surrounded by a crowd, but there was so much intimacy in that moment. Suddenly, Raman's dad felt like home.

Releasing myself from his embrace, I wiped my tears and whispered, "Thank you," once more before leaving.

Everyone around us was watching: the guys from KOMA, Sasha, my friends, and other people. Everyone looked at us. This staring made me feel uncomfortable, and I put sunglasses on.

I walked back to Natasha, and she welcomed me with a hug. I broke down once more, and Natasha wrapped her arm around my shoulder as we made our way toward the exit.

CHAPTER 12

April 2015–May 2015

Returning to Miensk, I couldn't wait to see Viera and tell her everything. I already texted her, saying that something crazy had happened but couldn't give her all the details. In response, Viera, of course, bombarded me with angry emojis for leaving her on tenterhooks, but I needed to talk to her in person. Too much was at stake, and I had to plan my actions thoroughly. I was absolutely out of my mind and couldn't think clearly.

We had chosen to meet at Manufaktura, and as I approached the place, I spotted Viera already there. The outside world had succumbed to the embrace of darkness, yet the terrace basked in the soft, rosy glow of the signboard. No one else was in sight except the two of us. I gave her a wave, signifying my plan to grab a coffee inside before joining her at the terrace. She nodded and returned to her phone.

Inside the cafe, I ordered the coffee and stood there waiting by the counter. The room was alive with the ambient chatter and sporadic laughter of patrons.

As I stood there, I got a flashback from the time when I sat beside Raman on a couch, with his arm gently resting on my lap. The mere recollection sent shivers through me, concealed beneath my sweater.

The barista handed me the coffee with a cheerful, "There you go." I secured the lid and stepped outside.

The transition from the warm, well-lit coffee shop to the chilly darkness of the evening, even though it was only 7 p.m., was stark. I walked over to Viera, put the coffee on the table, and gave her a hug.

"What's up?" I asked, taking a seat on a high bar stool.

"You tell me! We're not here to discuss my life. Tell me everything, Janina!" she responded with a laugh.

I started telling her the story, describing every single detail of that night, from the very moment of arriving in Mahilyow and not knowing what was going to happen but being so sure that something definitely would. I got so caught up in the tale that I forgot about my coffee, continuing with the description of meeting Raman—the way he looked at me, our conversation, and the moment he put his arm on my lap. My voice trembled with emotion as I reminisced about that moment. It was still hard to believe it had really happened, as if I couldn't entirely grasp its reality. But at the same time, I sort of knew that things would work out in the end.

The only thing that weighed on my mind was my early leaving. I couldn't shake the nagging feeling that I hadn't done enough, that I had missed something important. It was as if I should've done something but didn't. The scene of the bonfire was in front of my eyes. And behind it—Raman and his evil eyes. So cunning, so treacherous.

I was telling all these things to Viera, and a sense of regret for missing that moment engulfed me. I yearned to turn back time and do things differently. I knew I wouldn't have another chance to stand next to Raman, to talk to him like that. Like in that dream that I've seen the other night.

"Oh, come on! I'm sure you'll see him again!" Viera tried to make me feel better.

"I'm not sure… You have no idea how many fangirls chase him like that. He probably already forgot about my existence."

"Don't be ridiculous. You're underestimating yourself."

My naïve Viera. She always believed in the goodness of people and thought it was just my self-doubt.

"He followed you on Instagram and added you on Facebook. That's big!" She burst into laughter and added, "And he recognized you! He knows who you are and remembers you. I'm sure he'll text you!"

Viera's words touched me, and I couldn't help but smile at her cuteness. Jesus, she was so naïve, so naïve. She had no idea what kind of person Raman was.

We stayed there for a while, talking and gossiping until the late-night chill reminded us of time.

"Ugh, it's getting so late. I have to get going." Without waiting for my answer, she got off the chair and looked at me with impatience.

I removed the plaid shawl from my shoulders, and the freezing air sent a shiver down my spine. We cast one last glance at our chairs to ensure we hadn't forgotten anything before leaving.

We strolled toward the metro and decided to skip Niamiga station and walk straight to Frunzenskaja. It was dark and chilly, but the streets remained bustling with people. We walked in silence, that comfortable kind where words weren't necessary to fill the void. I smiled. Returning to Miensk had left me feeling melancholic, but Viera's presence always had a way of brightening my spirits. A simple cup of coffee and a chat with her were enough to heal my anxiety.

As we entered the station, I heard a message ding. I glanced at the screen and saw "Mr. Krasouski." Oh, fuck… I looked at Viera in shock.

"It's him…"

"What did he text? Tell me!"

"Just a laughing emoji." I was confused.

"I told you this was going to happen!" She beamed.

I had no idea what to text him back. To be honest, I didn't even want to think about it. My mind felt scrambled. He had actually texted me. HE TEXTED!

After bidding farewell to Viera, I found a seat on the train, and the reality of the situation sank in again. I rechecked my notifications just to assure myself that it wasn't a dream. But there it was, his message, confirming he had indeed reached out.

Only a few hours later, after I had returned home, I managed to put myself together and started thinking about what to reply. Seriously, what to reply? Who the hell sends just an emoji? What's the point? Anyway.

I stopped pacing the room and settled onto the edge of the bed. Opening the message, I saw the entire chat history with him. We had a history.

As I began scrolling through the messages, memories started to resurface—it was about tattoos. I begged him to make one for me. Oh, Jesus, that was embarrassing!

I locked my phone and collapsed onto the bed. All of a sudden, the anxiety that had gripped me earlier disappeared, and I giggled. That was quite a coincidence. I wondered if he had seen those messages, too. Maybe that was the reason he sent that emoji!

<

Yo! What's up?

You saw our previous message history?

hehe

I hit the send button and suddenly felt so confident about my actions. He appeared online and replied the same second.

>

Nope. Did you?

<

Yes, I've just read them all

I chuckled. A few minutes later, he messaged me again.

>

Concert in Chechnya

I'm tripping and saluting Sieg Heil!

WTF?

Then, he sent me a video of a schoolboy rapping by a chalkboard. What a fun conversation. I didn't know how to feel about it. Raman's attention was appealing, but the talk itself had no sense at all.

I tried to make conversation and ask him something normal but didn't get any adequate response. Every message was like the ravings of a madman. He had this huge wall protecting him from letting anyone in, from letting me in.

The conversation gradually fizzled out, and I worried he would never text me again. I just knew he wouldn't. I tried to come up with something original to text him so he would keep messaging me. I was so stupid. In the end, I think, I was texting him exactly the same stuff as everyone else.

Raman rarely texted me first after that day, but when I reached out, he always replied, shared stories, and made me laugh, making it feel as if we were friends.

One time like that, we were chatting about random things when he suddenly got quiet. He sent me another message a couple of hours later.

> *Sorry I'm so slow*

> *I'm writing. Almost done.*

Are you writing a play about your life hehe

> *Nope, girl. I'm writing music.*

> *It's for a video invitation to our concerts*

> *Hold on, I'll show you soon*

A few minutes later, he sent me a music file. I don't remember my feelings about the music itself, not sure if it really touched me then as it does now, but I was so happy because he sent me the track before it was out. He shared it with me. I felt so special.

"That's a nice one!" I said to him and got back to the things I was doing.

Later that day, I realized what a fool I was. He never answered my message. No surprise! I could've done better.

Trying to fix my miss, I texted him again late at night. "Are you guys having concerts anytime soon?" I wanted to see him so badly, but I couldn't say it to him.

He wasn't answering the message, and I worried he probably thought that the only thing I needed from him was to get free tickets to his concerts. But I didn't know how else I could get closer to him. I couldn't even invite him for a coffee. I didn't know why. Maybe I was shy, maybe afraid of rejection, or maybe I feared all the things this meeting could lead to. I just couldn't ask him directly even though he was so close to me then.

I needed to keep this conversation going. I couldn't lose this connection. I grabbed my phone again and, to my surprise, saw that he had actually responded, informing me about an upcoming concert in Miensk. I opened the message and saw he was still typing.

>

It's hard to call it a concert…

buuuuuuuut

we'll get smashed!

<

Mmm I love that!

Wanna get smashed hahaha

>

Well, then come to Viciebsk as well

All the craziest shit will be there!

We'll get smashed for real!

<

Daaaamn, I'd love to come but I don't know anyone there

I've never been to Viciebsk and it feels weird to go there alone

Even to get smashed for real haha

>

Well, you know me

<

Yeah, right, your presence on the stage will
help me a lot lol

>

You wanna ride a pony? haha

When I was a kid, I just hopped on the
train and smashed that pussy

And didn't give a fuck where I was

<

Lol I did that too

Don't make me look like a princess

In response, Raman shared the video he was working on, in restricted access. Just for me. This time, I tried to take the best of the situation and praise the sensitive soul of an artist by sending him tons of compliments, but I've never heard back from him.

Days passed, and I struggled to decide whether I should risk it and go to Viciebsk or not get involved with this at all. Raman's continued silence only compounded the uncertainty, heightening my anxiety. It made me want to give up on everything, but at the same time, it made him look even more attractive and impossible to reach. Ugh, what are you doing, Janina?

One morning, as I awoke already feeling drained from the incessant worry about everything related to Raman, a message from Natasha lit up my phone. She informed me that a bunch of Mahilyow people, including herself and Pasha, were going to the concert in Viciebsk. A wave of excitement rose from the bottom of my tummy.

It also somehow made me feel more at ease regarding our relationship with Natasha. Lately, it felt like she didn't really want to spend time with me and all these people together. Whenever Raman's name came up, she seemed to withdraw. I didn't know why, but I clearly felt her attempts to separate hanging out with me and with the trap gang. Then again, maybe I was just overthinking things, as usual... In any case, now she invited me to join, and I didn't care about the reason that had made her do so.

And there we were, squeezed into a minivan: Natasha, Pasha, Alesia, and me, along with four guys I hadn't met before, embarking on our journey to Viciebsk.

Alesia was nervously scrolling through Facebook and Instagram, searching for proof of Mikola cheating on her the previous night. No one knew precisely what had happened, but rumors were swirling that he had spent the night with some woman at Miron's apartment while others were getting drunk in a bar. Mikola wasn't answering Alesia's phone calls, and I couldn't help but ponder how frustrating it must be to date a popular musician. Gone was the assertive woman we knew; now, she was tethered to her phone, her gaze darting anxiously as she scrolled through images. Never trust band guys.

I felt a sense of relief when we finally reached Viciebsk, and I could get out of the car and escape the stream of hate and anxiety coming out of Alesia. Even in her calmest moments, her presence could be daunting, let alone when she was embroiled in an argument.

As soon as my feet hit the ground, I straightened my back, stretched my arms, and let out a sigh. I had my own reasons to worry. Should I message Raman to let him know I was there? Well, it was almost certain that we'd end up at the same party since the plan was to get together with Mikola and the rest. One thing I knew for sure was that I had to get drunk. Otherwise, my anxiety would fucking kill me.

I slid open the van door and peered inside. "Yo, guys, are we going to get booze?"

Pasha raised his brows and asked, "What do you wanna drink?"

"I don't know, whiskey probably?"

He idly moved in his seat, searching for a bag underneath. After he pulled it out, he crawled out of the car and stood in front of me.

"Alright, whiskey for you, brandy for the rest."

He pulled up the hood of his hoodie and walked away. Watching him disappear into the distance made me feel a sense of warmth. He was one of these people who were always there for you, helping you out with stupid asks and supporting you in any difficult situation. Not that the whiskey situation was especially difficult, but it calmed me down to know I'd get a chance to relax before we would head to the venue.

Settling back into my seat, I observed Alesia engaged in a heated conversation on her phone. The moment I entered the car, she turned away toward the window, shielding her face from view. All I could see was the gleam of her blond hair tied in a slender ponytail. With animated gestures, her long pink nails punctuating each word, she was angrily whispering into the phone which left no doubt that Mikola had been found and was now listening to the tirade about the irresponsibility and foolishness of his actions. He probably wished he had stayed missing for a little longer.

I caught sight of Pasha's pink hoodie in the distance. Hurry up, bro... A scared girl needs some alco-support...

He got in, shivering from the cool, damp weather.

"There you go." He handed me the bottle of whiskey. "Sorry, no glasses."

"Ha-ha, that's quite alright." I looked at the bottle in confusion. "I think I'll manage."

People in the back giggled.

I opened the bottle and took my first sip. My face contorted as the alcohol reached my taste buds. I wasn't used to drinking plain hard liquor.

As the car started moving, slowly rolling out of the courtyard, Pasha turned to me from the front seat.

"Janina," he said, "I'll talk to Mikola about your pass."

"What do you mean?"

"I'll ask him to put you on the list."

"Oh shit, I didn't even think about it!" I felt sick in the pit of my stomach. "Do you think it's not too late to fix it?"

"Will see. Otherwise, I'll just buy you a ticket. Don't worry."

What a guy, I thought and smiled.

We were already parking near the club when we noticed a taxi pulling over by the entrance. The door swung open, and Mikola,

Siargei, and Sviataslava climbed out of the car. My heart sank. I didn't want to see her and Raman together again.

Mikola and Siargei spotted us and made their way to our car, yelling and waving. They were wearing absurd fur coats over their bare bodies and carrying champagne bottles and wads of cash. We all burst into laughter. The scene looked utterly ridiculous. We joined the group and strolled together toward the entrance.

"Yo, bro," I heard Pasha talking to Mikola. "Can we put Janina on the list as well?"

"Broooo, everything's gonna be fiiiine!" Mikola laughed heartily and ran ahead.

Pasha looked back at me. "I'll buy you one, don't worry."

Upon entering the club, the first thing I saw was Raman talking with a security guard. He was wearing all black and looked serious. He glanced at our group and flashed a small smile.

Without waiting for anyone, Pasha went to another security guard holding a list in his hands and asked if he could buy a ticket from him.

"You're not on the list?"

"I am. It's for her." He turned back and pointed at me.

"She is with me," I heard a deep voice, and Raman stepped up next to me.

I smiled and said, "Thanks."

He smiled back and left. My knees got weak.

Inside, the venue was dimly lit and somewhat empty. A small stage in the corner was illuminated, while the rest of the space was shrouded in darkness.

Someone directed us to head upstairs. I raised my phone to light the way as I began ascending the stairs.

As I made my way up, someone flicked the lights on, revealing a spacious area with a few couches, plush chairs, and a table.

Natasha appeared beside me, removed her scarf, and whispered with a hint of annoyance, "This doesn't look like a club."

Indeed, the place looked weird.

"But you can drink your alcohol here!" I turned my head and saw the guy who had come with us from Mahilyow. Good point.

More people gathered in this warm, boisterous atmosphere. I tried to have small talks with a couple of people to just kill time, but my mind was far away from there. My mind lingered one floor below, listening carefully to the soundcheck and Raman's voice. *Why aren't you coming up here? Ugh…*

"You've met her, right?" The blonde girl I was talking to brought me back to reality.

"Uhm no, I don't think so…"

"Ah, okay. So, this chick was all over the place. I came to her…"

As soon as it was clear that my responses weren't necessary, my thoughts drifted back to thinking about the night. I was both nervous and excited. Deep down, I knew that things would work out one way or another. After all, we were here all together, and surely we'd stay together after the concert, right? Then, I remembered the train ticket I had purchased for the journey back home. Why did I even buy it? I was surely not going home. Well, whatever. Fuck the ticket.

The venue grew increasingly noisy as people gathered around the stage. The lights dimmed, and a thick cloud of smoke enveloped the stage. The crowd erupted with cheers and raised their hands.

I watched from the balcony, peering down at the excited audience. A sense of pride welled up within me. Raman's words, "She's with me," replayed in my head. *Yes, Raman, I am with you.*

As the guys took the stage, the crowd went wild. The lights flashed in rhythm with the beat, lighting up Raman's face and leaving it in darkness. My heart raced.

The concert passed by like a second. I couldn't stop smiling and felt so much warmth inside of me.

After the show, as people began to disperse, I went downstairs. I impatiently waited for Raman to come out, pretending to hang out with my friends while my heart thudded with excitement. Minutes stretched on, and my nervousness grew. The fatigue and weakness in my legs reminded me of the long day I had had. I sat down beside Pasha, leaning my head against the wall.

I spotted Raman walking toward us from the dark corner on the other side of the club. My heart skipped a beat when I saw his look. Something had changed.

He reached us, shook Pasha's hand, exchanged greetings with some of the other guys, looked me in the eyes, and said, "Thanks for coming." Then he left.

The next moment, I found myself sitting at the train station, waiting for my train. I felt shattered and abandoned, an overwhelming desire to cry welling up within me. Where did he go? To whom?

○

After returning from the trip to Viciebsk, I gave up my romantic hopes for Raman. It became apparent he wasn't the type of person I should see myself with, and I had no desire to be one of his one-night stands. What I had now was more than I ever dreamed about—I had space in his life.

Every week, I anxiously waited for Thursday, knowing that I would take Friday off and hurry to the bus station with a small backpack, escaping my dull life. After reaching Mahilyow, I would rush to Natasha's place to change before heading to Raman's, where I would stay until Monday morning.

In those few months, I noticed that Raman was never alone. Sometimes it was the couple who shared the house with him—a tall, burly tattoo artist, his girlfriend whose name I didn't remember, and their golden retriever. Other times, it was a random guy sitting by Raman's desk, enthralled as Raman passionately explained the intricacies of music through the colorful interface on his screen. Other days, two young girls, barely 16, would chat on the bench outside while Raman sat alone in the darkness of his room, staring at his monitor and clicking buttons on his black Yamaha keyboard.

There were times when I was lucky enough to have Raman spend hours with me, talking about music or watching documentaries together. At other times, I'd quietly lie in his bed, reading a book, or relax outside in the sun, subtly observing his life.

Raman's existence revolved around two things: music and drugs. Writing music was his main source of dopamine, and he turned to drugs when he couldn't write. He seemed to need at least one of these to survive.

As darkness fell outside, more people would slowly bring their tired bodies to the bonfire. I couldn't quite get it if Raman wanted to see them all. However, one thing was clear—if no one showed up, Raman wouldn't dare to go to bed alone.

Despite spending days and nights at his place, I wasn't sure if I truly understood him. I observed him from afar, much like I did when he was on stage, except this time, it was from a closer vantage point.

I knew something was bothering him, but he never found a moment to confide in me, and I lacked the courage to ask. It was easy to let it slide when we were partying every night.

My consciousness would briefly awaken when I was sober, but the truth was, I was never sober with him. Our days began with beers, afternoons with joints, and evenings with lines. And I loved it this way.

CHAPTER 13

August 2017

We found ourselves clustered in the narrow hallway of a restaurant styled as a fire department. All eight of us stood before the host, who anxiously scanned the reservation list, his finger tracing the names, and an occasional sigh escaping his lips. His performance felt somewhat absurd, given the emptiness of the room behind him. Eventually, he located an opening in his substantial notebook and invited us to follow him.

He led us to a table near the window and called a server to bring another table closer so we could all sit together. He gave us the menus and left us alone.

As I opened the first page, the mere thought of food made my stomach churn. I closed the menu and gazed at its cover, reflecting that it was probably a smart decision not to attend the wake. The idea of being there alone, amidst Raman's family and closest friends, seemed terribly uncomfortable.

"Janina!"

"Huh?" I snapped back to reality, finding the server waiting for my order. "Um... A glass of whiskey, please."

"Anything else?"

I momentarily drifted off again, only to be brought back by Siargei's exclamation. "Janina, God damn you! Order your food!" He chuckled.

"No, nothing else, just whiskey."

The server left, and I looked down at the empty table. I was afraid to raise my eyes and talk to others. Suddenly, I just wanted to get up and run away. Outside, further away from here.

I heard the guys chit-chatting, their voices distant and muffled, as if I were inside a bubble. I wanted so badly to break free from this bubble, out of this vicious mush, but I couldn't. I wanted to cry uncontrollably, but I couldn't. Breathe in. Breathe out.

I raised my eyes, trying to focus on Siargei. He was mentioning Raman's name. What was he saying? He gestured toward the sky, a smile on his face, and Katsia responded, "You think he's up there?"

Everyone burst out laughing. I laughed too. Raman was indeed quite on the opposite side from there.

Suddenly, Siargei glanced at me and said, "Janina hasn't said a single word since we left the funeral."

"Yeah, I was just about to say that," Katsia chimed in.

I wasn't sure what to answer. I looked at Natasha, saw her pitying look, and got a lump in my throat again.

Shortly, the servers came back and started setting the table with an array of dishes and drinks. The sight of the spread, including pork, potatoes, and crepes, made me wonder if we were celebrating something. I wondered how they could even think of putting food into their mouths. I wanted to vomit only by looking at it.

Pasha pulled out his phone, his face tense as he stared at the screen. "Mikola is still out of reach."

Natasha looked at him, concerned. "Have you tried to call Alesia?"

"Well, the last message from her was about Mikola being constantly hysterical. He would take sleeping pills with a glass of whiskey, pass out right after, wake up later, start screaming and crying, and everything would start over again."

Natasha's face got even darker. I was listening to this and couldn't believe it was really happening. This whole day felt surreal. But at least we were all together, coping with it, while Mikola seemed to be losing his shit. It was scary.

Siargei offered to visit Mikola and Alesia after we were done with food.

"Yeah, we should go check on them," Natasha agreed. Turning to me, she asked, "Honey, you joining us?"

"Um, no, I'm actually good," I replied, my words coming out as I struggled to find an excuse. "I better have a walk or something."

"Giiiirl, come on!" Siargei raised his voice. "We'll just hang there for a bit and then go home together."

I started mumbling the same excuses, unsure how to make them stop pressuring me, when Katsia intervened, "Jesus, stop pushing her! She's lost a friend and wants to be alone. That's normal!"

Natasha asked me quietly, "You sure?"

"Of course," I answered, thinking, Don't cry, don't even dare to cry.

We completed our meals in somber silence. When we were done, Natasha gently asked me again if I was sure about wanting to be alone. Forcing my lips to curve in a reassuring smile, I nodded. Natasha draped her arm over my shoulders and leaned her cheek toward mine.

○

After lunch, I decided not to wait for the guys' taxi and walked away with no specific destination in mind. I was feeling so empty. I no longer felt pain, and it was as though my soul had ceased to exist, while my body continued to function for reasons I couldn't understand. I desperately wanted to cry, but couldn't get a tear out.

I followed the bustling sounds of the city until I found myself on Piershamajskaja Street. So many things happened there. Everything reminded me of him.

As I gazed upon the familiar buildings and streets of Mahilyow, I couldn't grasp the reality of it all. What's the point of staying when he's no longer there? What's the point of living when he's dead? I couldn't imagine how I was actually going to continue living, knowing that he was gone. He just didn't exist anymore in this world. How is that possible? I couldn't find words to describe my emotions. My confusion. My incomprehension at what had happened.

My phone chimed with a message from Nasta, my university friend.

> *How are you, sweetheart?*

<
I'm alright

I texted her back and burst into tears.

I turned onto Miru Avenue and continued walking until I saw a path leading down to the river. The prospect of being alone in silence prompted me to take that route, away from the clamor of the city. I desired nothing more than to disappear, for everything to come to an end. Each passing minute felt like a slow, agonizing death, tearing me apart. I broke down and wept, my mind filled with memories of the last time I had walked this path from Raman's place, the last time I had been in Mahilyow. How many things had happened in that house… How many things could've happened there. It was my fault. I let it happen. I didn't save him. Only I was guilty. No one else was to blame.

I spent a few hours walking, talking to my mom on the phone, telling her about Raman's dad, and crying throughout. It surprised Mom that I was still crying, which triggered a twinge of frustration in me toward her for never truly understanding my emotions. How could I not cry? A part of me had just died. Forever. I didn't believe this pain would ever go away. How could she not see that?

I spotted a bench at a distance from the bustling crowd and made my way to it. After finishing the call, I took a seat, and opened Instagram. The very first post in my feed was Astap's post about Raman.

Raman was always a paradox. Unmoved by obituaries or sentimental displays, he glorified death and reveled in dragging others into his dark games. He spoke his mind without restraint. The notion of 'speak nothing but good of the dead' meant nothing to him. For a time, we were close—at least, as close as one could get to him. He was a difficult friend, frankly speaking.

There were two sides to Raman. One was a charming cynic, a life of the party, a walking musical encyclopedia. This Raman fascinated and attracted, making everyone feel alive. But then, there was the other side, a black vortex with no bottom, sucking in anyone who didn't run away in time. This side poisoned and destroyed, eventually making it impossible for me to stick around. Still, some people kept trying to find the goodness in him, and sometimes they seemed to succeed. Even though I eventually gave up, I can't deny the good moments we shared. Producing music for my album, going on tour, having tons of fun—those were some of the best times.

Raman was immensely talented, and his music remains a testament to that. Despite my disappointment in the man, I was never disappointed in his art. And despite his contempt for normal human emotions and hopes, he dreamed of being remembered for his music. Well, he achieved that.

You were an incredible asshole, Raman. I'll miss you.

For a moment, I was struck numb, as though I'd stopped breathing. It felt like Raman's ghost was standing in front of me. Astap saw right through him. I wasn't even close to knowing Raman as well as Astap did, but I knew it was the real Raman. I still remembered his eyes, bluish-grey, bright, clear. But also, I remembered his evil look during the moments when something was on his mind—these black, sparkly eyes. As if you were talking to the death itself.

I was rereading the obituary over and over again, trying to see Raman and understand him better. My mind wandered to all the people who adored him, those who continually sought his company, attempting to be close to him. Lyrics from a song from my childhood echoed in my mind: "We all loved you, but none of us managed to save you."

I suddenly felt so sad and broken, as if it all dawned on me once again. I wanted to go home, but I didn't have the keys and had to wait for Natasha.

<

Are you coming home soon?

The last thing I wanted was to head there, but I lacked the energy to walk around any longer. I called a cab, and in a few minutes, I was already on my way there.

As I neared the building, I spotted a few figures at the entrance. I realized it was Mikola, Alesia, and Pasha. The fact that Mikola was outside with them was somewhat surprising. I had imagined things being far worse.

I exited the cab and made my way over to them, hugging each of them.

I tapped Mikola on the shoulder and asked, "How're you?"

"I'm fine!" he exclaimed, and I realized how drunk he was.

I entered the building and ascended the stairs to get to the apartment. In the kitchen, I found Natasha and the others already well into their cups. It seemed like drinking was the only option I had at this point. I hadn't gotten sober since the last drink, but the truth was, I couldn't bear sobriety. I needed the constant embrace of alcohol to shield me from the overwhelming emotions.

We eventually moved to the living room. I settled onto the couch, curling my legs beneath me, and reached for the plaid on the other side to wrap around myself. The alcohol started to take its effect, bringing a welcome sense of relaxation.

Soon, the guys from the street came back and continued drinking. The room grew warm and stuffy. Mikola seated himself on the rug in the center of the room and spoke. It began as a light conversation, but gradually escalated into shouts and tears. Alesia sat down next to him, trying to downplay the situation and make it all look like a joke. Yet the tears grew louder. I felt like

Mikola desperately needed to talk it through, to be heard while no one was taking him seriously. Everyone was just laughing.

I wrapped the plaid around me even tighter and shut my eyes. I covered my ears with my hands, desperate to escape the tormenting sounds of Mikola's cries and the hysterical laughter of the others.

The next thing I knew, Natasha was gently shaking my shoulder, whispering, "Wake up, we're going home."

I rose slowly, feeling dizzy and lost, and followed Natasha to the exit.

O

The next time I opened my eyes, I saw the ceiling of Natasha's apartment.

Waking up is the worst. For a split second, you're not sure whether everything happened in reality or a dream, but suddenly, reality overwhelms you with a burden and pushes you onto the ground so hard that you can't breathe.

And you want to die.

CHAPTER 14

May 2015

"Alright..." Stas let out a heavy sigh, and I could tell it was his way of saying "yes." He had agreed to go with me to the NPL concert. I gave his curly head a playful pat and chuckled, to which he responded with a stern expression in his almost transparent blue eyes.

"I worry about you."

"Why?"

"He's not good for you."

My lips curled into a mischievous grin, and Stas just shook his head, returning his attention to the computer.

Jealousy! Of course, he wouldn't want his ex-girlfriend to date a fucking rock star. Strangely, the feeling of danger only fueled my affection for Raman. I knew he was bad for me, but I loved it.

I rose from the floor and headed to the bathroom. I felt too lazy to go back to my own place, so staying at Stas's seemed like a more appealing option.

I locked the door and stood in front of the mirror. Damn, what was I getting myself into…?

I leaned against the sink and examined my face in the mirror. He did find something in it. He found something special in my face. Or in my body. Or in my personality. What was it?

A sly smile danced on my lips as I pondered this thought. After flushing the toilet, I returned to the living room.

O

The following morning, I woke up early, shaking from excitement. The palpitations of my heart echoed loudly in my chest—*boom, boom, boom.* I glanced over at Stas, still peacefully slumbering beside me. But I couldn't stay still any longer. I needed to do something.

Swiftly, I hopped over him, snatched my hoodie, and made my way to the kitchen. There, I brewed a cup of coffee and settled by the window, the warmth of the mug seeping into my hands. I tucked one leg beneath me and smiled at the feeling of how perfect everything was. I anticipated the evening.

As I savored my coffee, I heard the bed creak and the soft sound of footsteps. Stas was awake. He entered the hallway, pulling on a t-shirt, and paused near the bathroom door before speaking.

"Morning. Why are you up so early?"

"I don't know. Too excited to sleep, I guess." I shrugged.

He sighed and disappeared into the bathroom.

I began contemplating what to wear for the concert. I didn't have many clothes to choose from at Stas's place, but I would probably manage to find something decent. If Raman liked me in the clothes, I wore that very first time, I was sure I could pull it off once more.

Stas reappeared from the bathroom and joined me in the kitchen. He made us toasts with cheese and another round of coffee, and we settled down on the dining bench. The gentle glow of the morning sun filtered through the window. I felt so peaceful and at ease.

I enjoyed being around Stas. It seemed like things were back to normal with us, and we managed to stay friends without the ups and downs that we used to have in the past, after our break-up. The day was warm and sunny, and I enjoyed the slow morning and the anticipation of the concert.

O

A few hours later, we started getting ready. After a couple of beers, we set off for the venue, which was just a 10-minute walk from Stas's place.

When we approached the club, the line was already a few tens long. I went ahead past the line to see if anyone from the band was there and could let us in. I entered the foyer, scanning the area, but no one was there. I showed our tickets to the security, and he stepped aside to let us in. Easy-peasy.

The concert itself seemed to whiz by in the blink of an eye. My body ached from dancing, but my soul was singing. Even Stas seemed to have enjoyed it, no matter how hard he tried to act like he was forced to join me.

As the lights came on, a wave of emptiness and uncertainty washed over me. I glanced around at the dispersing crowd, my anxiety growing. I looked at Stas in the hope of finding a solution, but he merely shrugged.

Panic set in. I couldn't come up with a single excuse to approach Raman. I felt trapped, torn between wanting to stay and the impossibility of seeing him.

The throng of people pushed us toward the exit. The galling noise of their laughter felt like nails on a chalkboard. I couldn't bear it any longer and decided to go to the bathroom in the meanwhile.

"Alright, I'll grab our stuff and wait for you over there." Stas pointed to a bench near the mirrors.

I nodded and navigated through the dense crowd, making my way to the stairs and descending to where the restrooms were located. Ugh, fucking people. I almost wished I had skipped the bathroom altogether.

The lower level was much quieter, with just a few people passing to and from the restrooms or loitering in the hallway. I pushed the door open and nearly collided with Sasha, our noses almost touching.

For a brief moment, we simply locked eyes, after which I screamed, "Hiiiiiiii!" I tried hard to look like a best friend forever and be incredibly nice.

"Oh, hi there!" she responded, stepping forward to hug me with her long skinny arms. "What's up? How was the concert?"

"It was awesome, really cool! What do you think?" I tried to play it cool, as if it wasn't a big deal for me.

"Yeah, the guys did it pretty well. Are you going backstage afterward?"

Sasha's question caught me off-guard. The way she asked it made it seem like a casual conversation, while I was trembling inside, my entire being screaming, "YES, PLEASE, GIVE IT TO ME!"

I glanced at her face and nonchalantly shrugged. "I don't know, to be honest. My friend is waiting for me. Why?" *Stay calm. Don't fuck it up…* Everything inside me treacherously shivered.

She answered casually, "Um, nothing special. We're just hanging out there, and I thought you might want to join."

"Ugh, I don't know... My friend is waiting," I said again, not wanting to leave Stas behind. But Sasha didn't seem to care about inviting him as well.

"Look, write down my phone number and call me if you decide to come. I'll let you in."

"Ok, cool."

I swiftly wrapped up in the bathroom and hurried back to Stas. I needed to talk about it.

I hadn't planned to call Sasha, but the chance of seeing Raman was driving me crazy. Sasha's invitation made me feel like a part of the crew, though I wasn't sure about going with Stas, and I'd never venture there alone—it was too scary.

I got up to the ground floor, and in a few big steps, reached Stas. He picked up my jacket from the bench, ready to hand it to me. I took it from his hands, not planning to put it on.

"Hey…" I didn't know where to start.

"What?"

"I ran into Sasha downstairs."

"And?" he asked abruptly.

"She invited me to come backstage."

"Well, go then," Stas responded, his expression carrying that familiar, hopeless look that always made me feel miserable. He didn't want me to go. And he probably felt sad that I was going to leave him there.

"Do you wanna go with me?" I already knew the answer, but I couldn't help but ask.

"What am I going to do there? I have nothing to do with people like them."

"People like who?" He suddenly started getting on my nerves. I was trying my best to be caring and got humiliation in return.

"I'm sorry, I didn't mean anything bad…" he quickly added.

"Whatever. We're going home then." I got sick of begging him, quickly grabbed my bag, and headed toward the exit. But Stas caught me by the hand and turned me back toward him.

"Fucking go there! You were dreaming about it, and now you have a chance! You'll regret it if you don't go…"

"I can't go alone! I'm scared! I'll be standing there alone like a fool and won't be able to say a word!" I frowned and looked him in the eyes.

"You won't be alone. You know Raman and this Sasha. That's already two people." He forced a smile.

"Yeah, maybe you're right…" I suddenly wanted to crawl under the blanket with Stas and fall asleep, wrapped in his arms.

"Call her!" Stas stood with his hands on his hips, staring at me impatiently.

"Fuck it," I muttered, grabbing my phone and dialing her number.

"Sasha? It's Janina. Well, I'm free now. Are you still there?"

"Yes! Come over. I'll meet you at the entrance." *Oh, shit.* I hung up the phone. *Fuck.* I was going backstage. I was shaking like crazy.

"It's gonna be fine!" Stas squeezed my shoulder and smiled.

"You're sure you don't wanna join?"

"No, I'm good. Have fun there." Suddenly, he looked so sad. He gave me a tight hug, turned away, and walked off.

I made my way back to the dance floor, on the lookout for Sasha. She met me at the backstage entrance, and we breezed past the security check.

The room where everyone was hanging was quite small and teeming with people. There were both familiar and unfamiliar faces, but Raman wasn't there. While I recognized some of these people from previous parties, I had never really talked to any of them.

I noticed Jauhien from KOMA and approached him to say hi. He looked at me with a momentary hint of confusion, probably unsure of who I was. He then launched into a rant about how shitty his life was. He was totally wasted and smelled like a junky. Well, at least I wasn't alone.

Discreetly, I scanned the room. It seemed like everyone was engaged in drunk conversations, fake laughter, and lackluster attempts at finding a hookup for the night. One guy was particularly zealous in his efforts, standing at the center of the room and breaking into an impromptu rap. It felt so pathetic, but the girls seemed to be enjoying his performance, gathering around him, laughing, and cheering him on. I couldn't help but cringe and wish someone would intervene to make him stop. What a dumbshit.

Out of the corner of my eye, I caught Raman's entrance. He wore a white t-shirt with dragonflies and a big smile. Our eyes met, and my knees went weak. He rushed over to me, wrapping me in his arms.

"Heeeey, girl!"

"Hi," I managed to mumble in response, my voice barely audible. I couldn't breathe. From his tight hug and from having his body so close to mine.

"How are you, baby?" Raman's hand still rested on my shoulder.

I looked up at his face and replied, "I'm good. And you?"

He knelt closer to my ear and whispered, "This asshole is getting on my nerves." Raman's warm breath sent shivers down my spine. He chuckled and added, "What a moron."

He gestured toward the guy who had been rapping a minute ago and was now filming himself playing with the tits of one of the girls.

I smiled with the corners of my mouth.

Raman released my shoulder but stayed by my side, observing the scene.

"Jeeezzz, girls, don't fuck this dork!" He laughed out loud and turned to me. "Come with me. There's a nice spot over there."

Taking my hand, he led me to the door he had come out of a few minutes earlier. In the darkness, I couldn't see anything until he opened another door, revealing a tiny room.

The room was no larger than a small walk-in closet and had minimal furnishings, just a large drawer taking up nearly half the space. The ceiling fixture didn't have a light bulb, and the only source of light in the room was a narrow thread of blue neon light encircling the room's edges. The dark red walls were covered with graffiti, band signatures, quotes, and various drawings. I gazed around, taking in the eclectic chaos. It was as if every performer at the club had left their mark in this room.

With a swift leap, Raman climbed onto the drawer and patted the surface, inviting me to do the same. I joined him in the cramped space. He tried to move over a bit to give me more room, but the drawer was clearly too small for two people. Although, I didn't mind sitting shoulder-to-shoulder with him.

I turned my head to look at him and leaned against the wall, my gaze fixated on his face. He noticed my scrutiny and smiled. The wrinkles on his face formed when he smiled, along with the dimple on his chin and countless small birthmarks tracing their way to the back of his head and down his neck. I wanted to touch his head and gently move my hand over the prickly stubble.

We sat in silence, smiling at each other. Raman placed his hand on my lap and gently squeezed my knee.

"Want a line?"

"Yep," I replied.

Raman hopped off the drawer, his fingers rifling through his jeans' pockets. After a moment, he triumphantly pulled out a tiny plastic bag containing white powder. We giggled like kids. Yeeei!

He poured a small mound of powder onto the surface next to me. Using a credit card, he meticulously divided it into two neat lines and then scooped out my portion onto the card. He gingerly raised it to my face, saying, "A royal treat for my queen."

Cautiously, I accepted it from his hand, trying not to drop a single grain of it. Raman leaned closer to the table and snorted his portion, and I followed suit. Closing one nostril with my index finger, I inhaled the line through the other.

Raman stood before me, closely watching my every move. As the euphoria surged through my veins, I leaned back against the wall, my eyelids heavy. I wanted to keep looking at him but struggled to keep my eyes open. A chill coursed through my nostrils and up into my head. I felt content and carefree, utterly unconcerned about anything or anyone. I couldn't help but smile.

"You good?" Raman's deep voice reached my ears.

I opened my eyes and gazed at him, his beautiful face before me. He leaned over the table, his hands on either side of my body, his crotch close to my knees. I smiled and touched his cheek. He smiled in return and drew closer to my face.

Just as I felt the warmth of his lips and my mind started to whirl, a door clapped open, and a loud male voice cut through the moment. "Yo, Raman, some dude is waiting for you over there."

I couldn't see the intruder's face, but already hated him. I looked at Raman. He sighed, looking into my eyes, and stepped back.

"I'll be right back." The door closed.

I drew my knees up to my chest, setting my feet on the drawer. Hugging my knees tightly, I stared into the darkness, wrestling with my thoughts. What am I doing? I'm fucking up my life. I can't, I can't do that. He isn't good for me.

I lingered there for several more minutes, but Raman never came back. I made my way back to the backstage room, and it was empty. The room was a mess, littered with garbage and empty bottles, but not a soul in sight.

I felt used.

CHAPTER 15

August 2017

I turned the key in the lock and quietly stepped into the apartment. Luckily, Mom was still at work. With a sigh of relief, I let my bag drop to the floor, kicked off my shoes, and made my way to the bathroom.

There, I quickly plugged the drain of the bathtub and twisted the faucet, letting the water flow. Impatient to soak away the day's stress, I wasted no time shedding my clothes and easing into the warm embrace of the rising steam, which sent shivers across my skin.

I cupped some water in my hand, feeling its warmth as I poured it over my shoulders. Gradually, I sank down, submerging my shivering shoulders in the comforting depths of the bath. A hot embrace enveloped my chest.

For what felt like an eternity, I stared at the cascading water, as if it were the most important thing in my life—something I couldn't tear my eyes away from. It was only when I noticed the water nearing the edges of the bathtub that I hurried to shut off the faucet.

I lay back down and threw my head back. My body was becoming weightless in the soothing waters. My chest gently rose and fell, its rhythm slowing down with every breath. I extended my leg above the water's surface, causing a plume of steam to ascend toward the ceiling.

Wishing to check my phone, I reached for it among the pile of discarded clothes on the floor, and a splash of water covered the mat. Shit, Mom will be pissed. I grabbed the phone and plunged back into the water.

Messages, likes, Facebook comments, "how are you's," "hold on over there's," "take care's," and all this shit I had no energy to read. I turned the phone off and put it back on the floor.

I wasn't sure how long I stayed there, but I realized it was time to get out when the water was barely warm.

I got out of the bathroom, shivering, and wrapped myself in a towel. Stepping gingerly over my scattered belongings, I walked to the bedroom. I pulled a t-shirt out of the closet and put it on my naked body. I closed the shades, crawled under the comforting embrace of the blanket, and passed out.

"Sweetheart!"

I rolled over, unsure what time it was.

"Daughter," Mom's voice carried a note of concern, and she pushed open the door.

I winced at the sudden brightness and instinctively shielded my eyes. "Mom, what?"

"Why are you not answering my calls?" She entered, switching on the room's harsh light.

"Mom, I'm sleeping! The light! I can't see!"

"Oh, baby, I'm sorry," she immediately switched off the light, "I was worried..." She made her way to me, taking a seat on the bed. She gently touched my shoulder and asked, "How are you?"

"I'm alright," I mumbled, my eyes still reluctant to open.

"How was your trip to Mahilyow?"

I took my hand off my face but still couldn't fully open my eyes.

"It was alright," I answered, squinting into the darkness.

"You're sure? You know you can talk to me anytime."

"I know. I'm sure. I'm alright."

No, I wasn't.

CHAPTER 16

May 2015

The morning after, I found myself on a rattling bus, headed to Mahilyow. It was evident that this bus had been in service long before the invention of air conditioning, as the air inside was oppressively hot and stifling. Nausea began to creep up my throat, unsettling me.

I put my phone away, worrying about my motion sickness. I imagined how the lump in my throat would break, and I would vomit on the lady who sat in front of me.

The scenery outside the window was depressing despite the yellow rapeseed flowers that made it look surreal. Oddly, the vibrant colors only intensified my growing anxiety.

After the concert last night, I was already on my way to the next one. I sighed, reminiscing about how close I was to Raman and how he just left me there alone. Like I was nothing. Zero. Yet, deep down, I held onto hope that I might see him again, praying for another opportunity to speak with him.

Suddenly, I felt the urge to text him. My mind was telling me not to—it'd be groveling, but my heart screamed, "fucking do it!"

<

So, how was last night?

>

idk lol

it was alco-bottom

I have never fallen this low 😄

I held my breath, awaiting the next message, hoping it would be more than this. Please, don't let this be it.

A ping signaled a new message.

>

Why didn't you go with me?

Oh my God, he cares about me!

I paused for a few minutes, contemplating my response. Thoughts raced through my mind, and I mulled over all the possible reasons for him to leave. There must be something! And now it proved he didn't just leave me on purpose!

I opened the chat and typed the response.

<

Why didn't you stay with me?

He immediately started typing his response. Please, let it be an adequate explanation, pleeeease.

>

Sweetheart, I was drunk like shit

I don't remember a single moment of last night 😄

That was it. I felt nauseous. "I don't remember a single moment" echoed in my mind, over and over again.

I hid my phone in my bag, leaned back in the seat, and closed my eyes. An internal battle raged within me, as I chastised myself for holding onto hope. What are you doing, Janina? No way this thing will work out for you… He is not a human. He is an asshole. Why do you keep forgetting it?

O

After a couple of hours of fitful napping, occasionally interrupted by the bus's abrupt jolts, I eventually reached my destination in Mahilyow.

As I got off the bus, my eyes quickly landed on Pasha's black car, parked beside a pizzeria. Our eyes met in the rearview mirror, and he quickly turned back in his seat and waved at me. I walked to him and sat in the front seat.

"Hey, girl," Pasha leaned in, offering a warm hug. "Natasha is inside ordering pizza."

"Nice, I'm starving!"

"How was the trip?"

"Oh, you know, long and tiring." I made a face. "But it's fine. I'm looking forward to the concert tonight!"

"Yeah, it's gonna be a good one." He looked in front of him, thinking. "I don't know, though, if we get a chance to get to the party. Too many high-class people are going to be there. Don't think we'll be among the invitees."

I frowned for a second, not sure what to answer. I mean, how could we *not* be invited when we know Mikola and also… I kinda know Raman.

I said, "Oh, it's gonna be fine. We'll come up with something."

The rest of the time we spent in silence. The things Pasha said puzzled me, and I didn't feel like maintaining a conversation.

The car door swung open, and Natasha climbed in, bringing with her the smell of pizza and the dense hot air from the street.

She said hi to us and squeezed my shoulder. "How are you?" Natasha asked gently.

"All good, excited about tonight!"

"Yeah, let's hope it all works out."

Pasha started the car, and we slowly rolled to their place. He turned up the music, skipping through songs one after another.

"Wait, wait, back," I said after catching the beat of the NPL song.

Pasha chuckled and cranked up the volume.

And there we were, driving through the city I loved, windows down, NPL blaring at full volume. A feeling of ease filled me up, making me believe that things would indeed work out.

Shortly after, we found ourselves on the floor of Pasha and Natasha's apartment, indulging in pizza. Pasha got up and walked to the kitchen, licking off grease leftovers from his fingers. He swung open the fridge and grabbed three cold beers. He gave us a look, meaning to ask if we wanted the drinks, to which Natasha shook her head no, and I said "mm-hmm" and set aside the pizza.

Pasha handed me an already-opened bottle, and I swilled the cold beer. We were chatting about random stuff, but I couldn't distract myself from worrying about the concert. I tried not to let my hopes soar too high, fearing disappointment if the night didn't go as planned.

Once the pizza had disappeared, Pasha gave Natasha a quick peck on the cheek and stood up.

"Time to go. Have to make sure everything is set up in the club before NPL guys arrive."

"See you there," Natasha answered.

"What time will you guys come there?"

Natasha and I looked at each other. I shrugged, "Maybe by 5?"

"Good. Text me when you're there, and I'll let you in."

He put the shoes on, waved at us, and left.

Natasha rose and began tidying up the mess on the floor.

"Wanna have some tea and then start getting ready?" she asked, standing in the kitchen's doorway.

"Mm-hmm."

While Natasha clanged around in the kitchen, I moved the pillows and other stuff onto the couch and slid the coffee table closer.

The kettle hummed and eventually clicked off. I heard Natasha pouring hot water, followed by the cupboard door opening and a rustling of paper. She slid the door wide open and came in, holding two plates of cookies. She put them on the table and went back for the tea.

"Niiiice, looks so yummy."

She didn't answer and only smiled, looking at the cups she was holding.

I asked, "Hey, wanna watch that girl's show about life, relationships, and stuff? While we're getting ready, I mean. You know that show? I mentioned it some time ago."

"Yeah, let's watch it!"

As I searched for the show on YouTube, Natasha sipped her tea. I clicked play and finally felt calmer. The room wasn't quiet anymore.

O

5 p.m. We were in a taxi approaching the club. A line of teenagers extended all the way down the street. We got out of the cab, and while the evening wasn't particularly cold, the air

felt much fresher than when I had first arrived. Although, I was still sweating from the anxiety and couldn't help it.

Natasha and I bypassed the lengthy queue and made our way directly to the entrance doors. We called our names and entered the club. After ascending three floors, we found ourselves at the main entrance. I pulled the heavy door and walked in.

It was pretty quiet inside. I could discern voices, but none I recognized. The soundcheck hadn't started yet, and I wasn't even sure if Raman was there.

I quickly checked my makeup in the bathroom and rejoined Natasha. She headed for the stairs leading to the second floor, and I followed her.

The space was completely empty on the second floor except for the chill-out room. Its door was shut, but I could hear the voices inside. Was Raman there? I couldn't understand.

Pasha was behind the bar, cleaning up the counter.

"Oh, hey, girls!"

"Hey," I replied, and Natasha leaned over the counter to give him a kiss.

"What do you guys wanna drink? Whiskey?" Pasha looked at me, and I smiled in response. "I got you."

He mixed my drink and handed it over to me.

"Are they already here?" I asked Pasha.

"Um, yeah, I think so. Mikola is here, and Miron is here too. I haven't seen Raman, but he must be in the chill-out. We can go there to say hi if you want to?"

"Ah, no, I'm good," I replied and took my glass with me as I made my way to the balcony to see what was happening downstairs. It was still relatively quiet, with just a few people wandering around.

My hands were already shaking with the knowledge that Raman was just a few steps away from me. Should I actually go there and say hi? Ugh, no, I can't. He'll come out here, anyway.

A sudden burst of static from the speakers caught my attention, and Raman's voice filled the air. He recited the lyrics from their latest song, devoid of any musical backdrop. The absence of music intensified the lines about hating people, casting a somber tone, until Raman's boisterous laughter abruptly pierced the air.

"Dude, the sound is bullshit! Do you even hear me?"

I held my breath, trying to understand where exactly he was. The stage was below the balcony where I stood, and I couldn't see anything happening down there. But I needed to see if he was coming up here.

"Hey, Janina!" Pasha called out.

I looked back at him. "Huh?"

"Try this," he said, handing me a glass of coke.

"Thanks, but I haven't finished mine yet."

"Take this one. You'll like it," Pasha grinned.

I took a sip and felt nothing special, but that sly smile made it clear that there was something mixed into the drink. It wasn't just coke, and there definitely wasn't alcohol in it.

I heard footsteps behind me, and as I turned my head, I saw Raman approaching us. With a few large strides, he closed the gap, wearing a wide, welcoming smile on his face. He greeted Natasha and me with brief hugs and... left.

Natasha looked down at my shaking hands and turned away. Of course, she understood everything, but what was the point of talking about it with her? She would never support my attempts to get closer to him. My only hope was tonight. I hoped so much that we'd end up at his place again…

The audience's euphoric screams filled the air. I peered down at the dance floor, where the first few rows were obscured by smoke. The rest of the crowd raised their hands, shouting in anticipation while gazing toward the stage.

"Yo, yo, yooooo," Miron's voice reverberated through the venue.

The audience replied with fervent screams.

The first beats of "I Need More Money" kicked in, and the crowd went wild.

I glanced at Natasha, hoping we could dive into the dance floor together, but all she gave me was a slight smile, nothing more.

"Wanna find where to stand?" Natasha asked.

"Sure," I answered, angry with myself for not being able to go and dance alone.

As we approached the stairs leading down to the dance floor, it became clear that every available space downstairs was jam-packed. People even stood on the stairs, making our passage almost impossible.

We forced our way through the crowd and managed to secure a spot on the stairway. Natasha nudged me forward so I could stand by the rail, then squeezed in next to me. We exchanged glances and shared a giggle.

I turned my head back toward the stage, and my heart raced. This was exactly where I had stood the first time I saw him.

After what happened last night and all this texting, I felt much more confident. I didn't see anyone around. I was only watching him as he strolled, danced, pulled faces, shouted, and laughed. Oh, Christ, I was so crazy in love with him…

Suddenly, he glanced in my direction and smiled. I reflexively smiled back. That must've been a random look, huh? There was no way he could see me in this sea of faces. Yet, he smiled again, and I chuckled. No fucking way.

The song ended, and someone from backstage handed Raman a small towel. He wiped the sweat from his face and locked his gaze directly on me. At that moment, I was certain he had seen me. And he was as excited to have me there as I was. *Fuck you, bitches, this man is mine.*

The slow intro of "Better than my iPhone" started, and the crowd erupted in screams. Raman stood there, his hands wrapped around the microphone stand.

He started singing, and his gaze returned to me, this time holding for a much longer moment. His eyes were directed at me as he smiled his sly smile, his devilish eyes dancing.

During the final lines, while singing the lyrics "You are better than my iPhone, so I'll send you my love in a text," something unbelievable happened. Raman let go of the microphone stand and made a heart shape with his hands, looking into my face.

With peripheral vision, I saw how people on the dance floor turned their heads up to me. It caught me off-guard so much that I didn't react at all. My face bore a confused expression.

Raman's eyes were still on me as people kept raising their heads and then quickly averting their gazes. Inside, I was quaking with emotion, struggling to accept that it had actually happened and not just in my mind. I scratched my head in confusion.

A few songs later, the concert was over. The band made a quick exit, darting through the crowd and exchanging high fives with fans as they went. They passed behind me and vanished into the chill-out area.

I kept my eyes fixed on the closed door, battling with the desire to follow them. Ugh, no, I can't. So silly. It was so easy, and I just didn't go. Instead, I waited for others to make things happen for me.

Realizing that Natasha was no longer by my side, I heaved a sigh and made my way back to Pasha's bar.

Just as I thought, Natasha was standing by the bar checking

her phone. She saw me and smiled. I came by, and she wrapped my shoulders.

"You look sad. You feeling alright?"

"Yeah, all good."

Pasha joined us and asked, "So, how was the gig? I came to the balcony a couple times, and it looked dope, huh?"

"Oh yeah, it surely was dope!" I chuckled, recalling how Raman had shown me a heart. "What's up for tonight?"

Pasha switched his attention to the couple standing by the bar. "Two mojitos?" He keyed in the order on the bank terminal and handed it to the man.

"I don't know." Pasha said, and I realized the answer was directed at me. His gaze and words, coupled with his sad expression, made me feel queasy.

I kept looking at him as he finished serving the guests until he came closer to us and said, "It looks like the party tonight will be a private one." He leaned forward, and Natasha and I reflexively did the same. "There's some girl coming from Moscow, apparently bringing drugs. I don't know why it's such a big deal, but this is the first time Mikola hasn't said a word about it. So, apparently, members only."

"Fuck." I sighed and straightened my back.

"I know. I'm sorry."

O

The next moment, we found ourselves in a taxi heading home. Pasha had taken a "tiny sip" of whiskey that had somehow left him struggling to walk straight.

Natasha and I sat in the back seat, with Pasha beside the burly taxi driver. I was too upset to join their chit-chatting. All I could hear was my own deep breaths and sporadic laughter from the front seat. What am I supposed to do? I was so despairing that I was about to cry.

I reached for my phone. No new messages. *Hah, what did you expect, Janina? You thought he'd text you and ask you to come over? So silly.*

I tapped on Ian's name and started typing a message.

<

I'm high

I have no idea what it was :(

But it feels so fucking good hahaha

Oh Ian, you'll never guess what Raman did tonight

You know, I don't talk too much to him

He just came to me to say hi before the concert

BUT

During the concert I was standing on the stairs right in front of the stage

They were singing 'and I'll send you my love in a text'

He looked at me and showed me a heart shape with his hands!!

I thought it was probably for someone else, told my friend about it, but she said 'no, it was for you. I saw that he showed it to you'

Fuck, I just don't understand

We've just left and I haven't seen them since

No reply. Well, I didn't expect any, to be honest.

The car came to a halt. I stepped out and closed the door behind me. Natasha made her way to the entrance door without even looking at us, and we trailed behind. When I opened the apartment door, Natasha was already sitting on the floor, hugging one of the cats.

"Wanna have some tea?" she asked.

Tea? Seriously?

"Nah, I'm good," I answered, trying to stay calm, and turned to Pasha, who was struggling to take off his sneaker that apparently was stuck on his foot. "Have you heard anything from Mikola?"

Pasha gave up on the sneaker, straightened up, and pulled out his phone. "No, nothing." He looked at me and shrugged.

Finally managing to shed both his shoes, he locked himself in the bathroom. I lay down by Natasha's side.

"Maybe we can cook something tonight?" Natasha suggested, turning to me and awaiting my response.

The peaceful look on her face suddenly made me hate her so much. Couldn't she at least act like she sympathized with us being sad and stop acting like no one even cared?

"Let's see. I'll check with Raman and see what the plan is."

Natasha paused for a second with her mouth half open, as if she were about to say something, but wasn't quite sure if she had heard me correctly.

I wasn't sure either. I definitely didn't plan to text him, but there was no turning back now.

<

Ramaaaan, the gig was insane!

Thank you so much!

>

I burst into laughter and showed Raman's response to Natasha. The bathroom door clicked, and I hurried over to Pasha to show him the message. He examined the screen and broke into a smile.

"What should I answer him?"

"I don't know," he mused, scratching his head. "You think we have a chance of getting in?"

"Why not? At least he's answering messages! I'll ask anyway. Nothing to lose." I laughed heartily.

<

Are you guys planning anything tonight?

>

Will find out soon

<

Text me if there's something

I'm going home tomorrow and wanna do something stupid tonight lol

>

Okie dokie

Silence descended, and with each passing moment, anxiety dug deeper into my stomach. The three of us huddled on the couch beside the phone. Two of us clung to hope, praying for a positive answer, while the third one looked like she didn't give a shit. The stakes felt impossibly high, as if my whole life hinged on this night. I started feeling desperate, thinking that nothing good would come out of it. We had to give up…

Ping!

I breathed out. Holy fuck.

At the same moment, Pasha's phone vibrated.

"Mikola is asking if we're coming," he said, a jubilant grin on his face as he typed a reply.

Natasha grabbed her phone and said, "I'll call a cab."

I rose from the couch and headed to the bathroom to freshen up. I couldn't believe this was really happening.

A few minutes later, I heard a soft knock on the door.

"May I come in for a sec?" Natasha whispered.

I opened the door and stepped aside to let her in. She slipped in and quietly shut the door.

"I wanted to talk to you," she began.

"Mhm," I replied, turning my attention back to the mirror to continue my makeup as she spoke.

She stood behind me and looked at me in the mirror. "Janina, what's your deal with Raman?"

I looked at her face and didn't see a single sign of a smile, anger, or indifference. I saw concern and worry.

I closed the powder box and put it on the sink. "What do you mean?"

"Do you like him? I'm just trying to understand what exactly you're trying to get from him."

I couldn't stop the smile on my face but tried to answer as indifferently as I could. "I do, Natasha. I like him. But it's not like I fell in love with him. I just enjoy spending time with him. You know how much fun he is."

She wrapped her arms around me and rested her chin on my shoulder. "Janina…"

"What? I mean, I know what kind of person he is. I'm not planning to marry him." I nervously laughed. "I'm just really enjoying it all, you know…"

"I know, baby. Just be careful, please. You won't even notice how he breaks you. So please, don't let it get to that point, okay?"

"Of course!" I covered her hands with mine in a sign of agreement.

We stayed like that for a few more seconds, after which she let go of my shoulders and said, "Well, let's get ready then. Do you have space for me by the mirror?"

"Sure," I replied, shifting makeup boxes and bottles to the side.

In a few moments, I was sitting on the couch, nervously waiting while Natasha was finishing her makeup. Pasha sat next to me, mindlessly flipping through TV channels.

"I'm finished!" Natasha stood in the doorway, wearing a smile.

Pasha and I exhaled in unison and proceeded to the hallway to put on our shoes and head out.

As we stepped into the darkness of the driveway, I shivered and straightened up the collar of my jacket. We stood there in silence, waiting for the cab to arrive, and a sense of growing excitement welled up inside my stomach. The feeling was so warm and pleasant that I wanted to stay in that moment forever. The cold air, the deep blue night, the clear sky, and the distant sounds of a nearby party in one of the apartments. I couldn't help but smile.

Pasha's eyes fixated on a spot ahead, his gaze slightly unfocused with a frozen look of confusion. Yo, bro, relax, I thought to myself and smiled.

Natasha's face was bathed in the glow of her phone's screen. She was engrossed in scrolling-typing-scrolling-typing, likely dealing with clients eager to book appointments for her eyebrow treatments.

The courtyard illuminated as the taxi approached, slowly making its way past the parked cars. We all paused our activities and stepped back to allow the cab to stop. We got straight into the car and quickly shut the doors.

While Pasha engaged in a small talk with the driver, I leaned in closer to Natasha's ear and asked, "Who's that Moscow girl?"

"Well, everything I know is that her last name is Kraeva. That's what everyone calls her. A girl from Moscow, a daughter of some super-rich parents. Not sure what she's doing, but people regard her as a drug dealer. Who else can be Raman's friend?" She laughed, and I giggled too.

All the fuss around this girl puzzled me. Should I be jealous of her?

After about 15 minutes, I began to recognize the neighborhood. The tiny grocery store, surrounded by towering apartment buildings. The crowded, dimly lit parking lots filled with cars stacked upon cars. The dead-end street where we'd have to exit the taxi and continue on foot until we reached the cliff. The descending staircase, the murmur of voices, and the glow of a bonfire. It was all so familiar. A lump formed in my throat, but I continued down the stairs.

The gathering around the fire seemed similar to the previous times, except that there were fewer girls.

After finishing the never-ending stairs, I headed straight to Raman. He was talking to a girl I'd never met before, but I figured it was probably Kraeva.

She was relatively short, barely reaching Raman's shoulder. Dressed in baggy jeans and an oversized hoodie left carelessly unzipped, her figure seemed to dissolve into the fabric. A dark t-shirt peeked out from underneath, adding to the illusion of shapelessness. Her short hair looked disheveled, framing a pair of big black eyes smudged with remnants of eyeliner and mascara. The spots on her clothes and the unkempt look made it hard to believe that she was a daughter of wealthy parents. As I swallowed, a sense of unease crept over me in her presence, but I continued walking toward them.

Kraeva noticed me first, and Raman followed her gaze.

"Hi there," I said as positively as I could and gave Raman a hug.

"Hi, girl," he answered.

I was about to turn to the girl, but realized she was gone. Instead, I spotted Miron standing nearby.

Scanning the scene, I noticed a lot of unfamiliar faces. Apart from Raman, Mikola, and Miron, there were Andrei, Siargei, two guys I'd seen in the club, and two girls, one of whom was presumably Kraeva.

The atmosphere wasn't as welcoming this time, or perhaps I just didn't feel confident enough in the presence of Miron and Kraeva. Speaking of the latter, she didn't leave Raman's side for a single moment, and he seemed to enjoy her company a lot. Every now and then, I could hear him laughing at her jokes, and she was clearly the center of attention.

I noticed a full plastic bag from a grocery store by one of the benches and decided to grab something to drink. Suddenly, all this fun wasn't fun anymore once I felt sober. I needed to catch up.

As expected, the bag was filled with beer bottles and two packs of chips. I sifted through them and picked out the most decently looking bottle. I cracked open the beer, causing the cap to pop into the air and disappear somewhere under the bench.

I took a seat and savored the first sip. The beer's taste reminded me of how thirsty I was.

I had no intention of spending the night watching Raman chat with some random woman, and I was on the verge of pulling out my phone when someone's broad shoulders blocked the light coming from the lamp above the house entrance.

"What's up, girl?" He took a step closer, and I could see that it was Andrei.

"Hi."

"You're hanging by yourself again?"

"Just chilling here. What's up?"

"Nothing. Just wanted to keep you company," he said, subtly adjusting his pants before sitting down next to me.

"Mhm."

He drew closer to me and tucked a strand of my hair behind my ear. I looked at him sullenly and saw his smug smile, the look of a person full of himself. It irked me for a moment, but then a feeling of contempt washed over me as I witnessed his desperate attempts to keep pace with the other guys in the group. It became clear that he must have been aware of his inability to ever truly catch up with them, and the realization must have been a bitter pill to swallow.

I quickly stood up and nervously looked for a spot where I could escape. Many people were gone somewhere, including Natasha and Pasha. Where the fuck are you, guys?

I stood quietly aside, shrouded in darkness, observing the few people who stayed by the fire. My mind was clear, yet strangely, the beer offered no respite from my anxiety. What's wrong with me, I thought, Why am I feeling so uncomfortable around them?

A raucous burst of laughter snapped me out of my thoughts. Raman and Miron stood together, guffawing at the expense of the guy seated on the bench—the nice, shy guy I had spoken to earlier that night at the club. He started muttering something, peering up at them from his perch. Before I understood what this was about, Raman and Miron burst into laughter again. Their faces were lit by the blazes of fire, which made their laughter seem even crueler.

Miron took a deep breath in an attempt to quell his hysterical laughter, wiping tears from his face. Stuttering from amusement, he quipped, "You really think that someone will be coming to *your* club if you continue this redneck bullshit you do at Cuba? Like, it wasn't a joke?" Miron threw his head back and laughed again. "OMG, what a moron!"

"G-guys…"

"Raman, did you hear that? This… little… faggot… club… MUSIC!" He put his head on Raman's shoulder, continuing to laugh.

Raman patted his friend's head and giggled, looking at the club guy. "Bro, that sounds like a good plan, actually. If you have your own club, you can even live there and finally move out of your parents'! Or you can even take your mommy and daddy with you! Oh, sorry, I forgot you don't have a daddy! Sad face…"

The guy on the bench sadly lowered his head. Not a single person came to his defense, and for a brief, heart-pounding moment, I held my breath, trying not to get noticed. As if any accidental move would make them switch their attention to me.

The courtyard got lit with light, drawing my attention toward its source. The house door stood wide open, and a dark figure cheerfully walked towards us.

Before I understood who it was, I heard the squeaky voice saying, "Yo, guys, wanna start off with some weed?"

In the darkness appeared Kraeva's face.

"Oh, fuck this bullshit," I heard Raman's loud voice. "We need some real stuff!"

"Real stuff! Real stuff!" Miron chimed in, gesticulating like a rapper.

"Pfff, whatever." She shrugged and turned to me. "Do you want a joint?"

She handed a hand-rolled joint to me, and I carefully took it.

"That's my girl!" Kraeva chuckled, retreating toward the house and shutting the door, casting the courtyard back into darkness.

Before I even thought about what I was going to do with the joint, Raman suddenly stood next to me with a lighter. I wrapped the joint with my lips, securing it there with the tips of my fingers, and leaned toward the lighter.

He lit the lighter, and I briefly looked up at his face. The orange light from the shivering flame was illuminating the dark spots of his face and, in a second, leaving them in darkness again. His eyes were fixed on the tiny flame, and suddenly, he shifted his gaze toward me.

"Is it good?"

For a moment, I looked at him and then started coughing like crazy. Raman smiled and hid the lighter.

"You okay?"

I nodded, trying to control the cough.

"Is it good?" he repeated.

"Yeah, not bad," I replied before finally taking a deep drag.

Warmth filled my lungs, and I handed the joint to Raman, exhaling the smoke slowly. He smoked a few puffs and handed the joint to the next person. I kept standing there in darkness, trying to feel the drug as quickly as possible, hoping to take control of the growing anxiety.

"Time to do real stuff!" Raman exclaimed, rushing over to me and draping his arm around my shoulders. "You're ready, baby?"

I grinned. "Ready for what?"

"You'll see!" With a gentle nudge, he pushed me toward the house, and I gave in to him, leading me there.

Raman opened the door and let me step in first. The sudden bright light blinded me and made it hard to navigate. The space felt both familiar and new at the same time.

I walked, following the sounds of voices and came into a bright pink room bustling with people.

Tall, black soundproofing panels covered the walls. In the center of the room stood a massive wooden table that housed a monitor, two laptops, a sound system, and tons of other gadgets I had no clue about.

On one side of the room, there was a bed. Natasha was lying there, staring at the phone she held above her head. Pasha sat on the other side of the bed, next to Miron. Two other guys were smoking near the window to the right. Ms. Kraeva stood beside the table with her back to us. She bent over the table as if she was scrutinizing its surface.

Raman eagerly sprinted toward Kraeva, rubbing his hands in anticipation. I couldn't quite discern what was on the table until Kraeva moved away, revealing two piles of white powder.

Raman caught my eye and broke into a smile. "Wanna try first?"

The question caught me off-guard, and I quickly answered, "Sure!"

He laughed. "You're a fucking psycho!"

I made a face and asked, "Why?"

"Who snorts something they don't even know what it is?" He burst into laughter again, and I felt uncomfortable, regretting my words. Well, no way back.

Gently, I nudged him out of the way and walked to the table. Kraeva remained in the shadows, standing by the table bathed in the monitor's light. Everything welcomed me to just go there and dive into the unknown.

Suddenly, a dark figure leaped right in front of me, snapping me out of my thoughts.

"Let me try first," said Pasha, leaning in for a moment and adding, "Come on, you don't even know what that is."

"As if you know," I teased him.

"I've tried too much stuff to be worried about it."

Without waiting for my answer, Pasha bent over, pinched one nostril with a pointed finger, and snorted one of the piles.

I was mesmerized, watching this whole action. Every second felt like an eternity as I imagined myself doing the same—the cool sensation I'd feel as the white powder entered my nostrils and crept up into the bridge of my nose, the lightness it would bring to my heavy body.

"HOLY SHIT! ARE YOU CRAZY, BRO!?" Following Raman's shout, the room suddenly fell into silence, and everyone froze.

Raman gaped at Pasha, a mix of shock and amusement on his face. Pasha stared off into the distance, looking entirely lost.

"He snorted the rest of the pile! Jeeezzz, bro, the line was yours but not the rest!" Raman dashed to the table, rifling through the stuff, trying to find the rest of the bags with the drug. "You better pray to God we have something left, or I'll fucking end you!"

He continued rummaging, muttering, "Jesus fucking Christ, this fucking idiot... Unbelievable..."

In an abrupt turn, he pulled out a square, transparent plastic bag containing the rest of the powder above his head. "We're saved!" Then he glanced at Pasha, who was now standing in the doorway as though he had been about to leave but had forgotten his destination. Raman said, "See you in space, bro! Be brave."

Natasha rose from the bed and cast a reproachful look at Raman.

"What did I do? He did it himself!"

Natasha draped her arm over Pasha's shoulder and led him

out of the room. In a few moments, the sound of the entrance door closing reached my ears. I hope he'll be fine, I thought.

The room filled with laughter and chatter, pulling me away from my concerns.

My gaze returned to the table. Raman and Kraeva stood there, welcoming me to taste the fun. This time, Raman cautiously set aside a narrow line from the rest to make sure no one messed up with the rest of the drug.

I walked to the table and leaned down to snort the thing. It felt exhilarating to be such a rebel, crossing the line.

Raman held my hair until I was done. I raised my head and breathed in deeper to feel the coolness of the powder traveling through my airways.

Then my gaze fixed on Raman. He looked at me with curiosity, waiting until it hit me. I broke into a smile, and he laughed in return.

I looked around at the people in the room. Everything was hazy. I yearned for freedom and fresh air.

I turned back toward the exit and slowly walked there, carefully making each step as if I did it too fast, I would lose the happiness on my way like pebbles out of my pockets.

I swung the entrance door wide open and stood there for a moment, trying to see who was sitting by the fire. I stood in the light of the lamp hanging above my head, with a wide, stupid smile on my face and squinted eyes, trying to focus. I noticed Natasha and Pasha sitting on one of the benches and walked to them.

"How are you?" I asked Pasha, scrutinizing his face for clues. He didn't look well.

"Um, I'm ok-kay… No worries, I'm gonna be fine…" Pasha stammered, struggling with each word. Natasha was stroking his head, but there was frustration and disappointment in her eyes.

Across the fire, I noticed three guys sharing a joint, engaged in a conversation I couldn't overhear. They all seemed gloomy and upset. What was wrong with them all?

I was about to go back inside when the door opened, and the noise from the inside poured into the courtyard.

The group stumbled out and walked toward us, laughing and shouting. In a matter of minutes, all the benches were occupied, and the atmosphere was filled with excitement, laughter, and merriment.

Raman stood beside me. I looked up at him, unsure of what to say, and he just smiled in return. With my peripheral vision, I subtly observed him, his hands in his pockets, jacket sleeves casually rolled up. It felt like he was doing the same, examining me in return.

Miron darted past us, wielding an ax, and disappeared into the nearby bushes.

"You fucking moron, what are you doing?" Raman's voice boomed.

Miron glanced back with a crazy grin on his face, swinging the ax wildly to demolish the dry bushes around him.

"Ah, I love this idiot," Raman remarked without looking at me.

I chuckled, entertained by Miron's antics as he wreaked havoc in the underbrush.

Suddenly, something touched the top of my head, and I flinched in surprise. Raman's hand was carefully picking bits of ash from my hair. *Breathe in. Breathe out.*

I raised my eyes slowly, scared to meet his gaze, and he just smiled. He gently blew the last of the ashes from my cheeks and then turned back to the crowd. I glanced around, wondering if anyone had seen it, but no one seemed to notice anything. Life continued as usual.

I started to turn toward the house, contemplating going inside, when Raman dashed over to me.

"Where're you going?"

"To the bathroom. Why?"

He breathed out, "I thought you were leaving."

"Awww," I teased, "Don't worry, baby boy. I'm not leaving you just yet." I smiled, flirting, watching him come closer to me and wrap his arms around my shoulders.

He hugged me tightly and whispered into my ear, "I don't give a fuck." A burst of laughter escaped him as he swiftly released my wilted body.

Confused, I turned around and made my way back to the house.

I came back shortly after and settled onto the bench facing the crackling bonfire. The warmth of the fire reminded me of how chilly it got outside.

The fire playfully tossed around tiny sparkles of light. I brought a beer bottle closer to my face, engrossed in examining its sticker. Someone's shoulder slightly pushed mine while sitting down next to me. I turned my head and saw Raman.

"You good?" he asked quietly.

"Yeah," I replied, turning my gaze back to the crackling fire, "Just feeling a bit lost, I mean, because of all this stuff." I looked back at him to see if he understood what I meant.

He smiled in return and started saying something. I couldn't hear a single word. I watched his mouth move, saw him laugh and gesture, but it was all lost in the white noise filling my head, leaving only his handsome face in my line of sight.

He continued speaking, slowly rubbing his hands, nervously looking at me, and then back at his hands. *Jesus, Raman, are you nervous, darling?*

His stuttering brought me back to reality for a moment, where I could hear the chatter of people around us, the crackling of the fire, and Raman's anxious words. I still couldn't understand what he was talking about, but I didn't even care. Feeling his presence was enough.

My drugged mind struggled to understand what was going on with him, but I knew I had never seen him like this.

Suddenly, he made a quick, convulsive movement, and his arm ended up on my shoulder. I chuckled, realizing how amusing it was. Raman, this cynic, rock star, and such a cad was just getting nervous because he didn't know how to hug me? I smiled and leaned against him.

As I gazed at the bonfire, feeling Raman's arm around my shoulders, I thought to myself that I had never been happier. I felt like I reached a height I had never even dreamed about before. I didn't need anything else. The happiness was tearing me apart.

I was thinking about us, imagining the ways we could date while living in different cities. Everything looked so perfect in my drugged mind. In reality, I was just high. But even now, I can say that I've never been happier than I was that night. I say that it was the best drug I've ever tried because it gave me a feeling of indescribable happiness. Although, I know it was Raman who gave me that feeling.

Just then, my phone vibrated. I pulled it out and saw Natasha's message.

>
So how's everything?

I raised my eyes at her. She was slyly smiling.

<
Try to guess lol

I don't wanna go home

>
Then stay 😄

I did want to stay so badly. More than anything else.

Another vibration and another message. This time from Ian.

>
You know it's love when Cupid's right next to it!

Looks like you're attracted to crazy guys like me and that Raman

And crazy guys are attracted to you

<
Iaaaan

>
Can I call you now?

<
I can't talk now 😞

Sorry

I'm high on something and don't want you to hear me like that

>
Good girl

On Friday I was offered cocaine

But I said no

As usual, Ian attempted to turn the focus onto himself. He wanted to show me he was also a bad guy.

In response, I forwarded him the screenshot of my conversation with Raman. Fuck Ian.

> *Baby*

I ignored the message.

> *Baaaaaaby*

Not going to answer.

> *What was the drug?*

< *I don't know*

> *Why did you snort an unknown drug?*

You're the same as me

I also did all this shit when I was your age

You know how I feel about you?

Like a gift or a chance

Just appreciate you so much

Like a miracle

< *Ian, I'm a horrible person*

> *Why?*

<

I just am

\>

Tell me what you feel

Why the fuck you snorted this shit??

Ugh...

<

I did it again

I don't feel anything

\>

When I see you, I'll fucking kill you!!!

I returned to reality and immediately noticed the curious gazes of everyone around us. Raman's arm still rested on my shoulder, but his attention had shifted to something beside us. I followed his line of sight and spotted Natasha playfully feigning a fist threat, as if warning him not to hurt me. Raman laughed and then returned his gaze to me to see my reaction. I chuckled and turned my head back to the crackling fire. The sudden silence made me realize that everyone else was now watching us intently.

"Would you like to stay longer?" Raman seemed not to notice the interest of others.

"Tonight?"

"No, I mean after tonight." He took my hands in his palms and gently rubbed them. "You can stay here as long as you want."

My response wavered, and I stumbled over my words, "Uh, I can't. I mean, I have to go home." *What are you saying, Janina? Shut the fuck up, stay!* "I'd love to, but I really have to go back tomorrow." His offer caught me off-guard. It paralyzed and scared me.

He released my hands and leaned back. He looked straight into my face and asked, "What is it that makes you have to go back?"

I stammered, "I mean… I have dogs that I have to take care of. In the shelter, I mean…"

He laughed and asked, "Dogs!?"

"Yeah… I really have to go tomorrow."

"Alright, I got you," he conceded.

Raman remained there for a moment, keeping his distance from me so that no single part of our bodies touched each other. I felt a sense of shame welling up within me. I wanted to take my words back but wasn't sure what I would say instead. I wanted him badly, but the possibility of staying alone with him horrified me. Nausea churned in my throat, and I swallowed hard in an attempt to quell the queasiness.

The sound of my swallow captured Raman's attention, and he turned to me. Our eyes met, and he offered a warm smile before resting his head on my lap. He wrapped his arms around my hips, nestled with his face buried in my lap.

For a moment, I felt shy and unsure about how to react, so I gently placed my arm on his back. Through his thin jacket, I could feel the warmth of his body, the rise and fall of his chest with each breath. I traced the small, round bones of his spine with my fingers.

I continued to stroke his back and leaned down, resting my head on his back. He held my hips tighter, and I could feel his breath warming my thighs. The nape of his neck was mere centimeters from my face, and I could hardly stop myself from moving closer and kissing it.

We sat in silence, in front of the crowd, absorbed in nothing else but the warmth of our intertwined bodies. The happiest I had ever felt.

His shoulders shifted, and I raised my head, allowing him to straighten his back. Raman stretched his body and then placed his hand on my lap, asking, "Move with me to Saint Petersburg."

He was looking at me, waiting for an answer as I anxiously scrambled for words. *No, I can't. Raman, I'm fucked up…*

"Ugh, I can't…"

"But why? I don't get it…"

"All my life is here. My family, my…"

"Dogs!" He laughed.

"Everything! I can't just quit everything and leave…" The more I spoke, the more ridiculous it sounded. I was using excuse after excuse, and Raman could surely see the fakeness of it all.

"Alright, I get it. It's cool." He grabbed my hand and shook it in reconciliation. My hand dangled limply in his hand.

"I'm feeling sleepy," I said, adding, "that shit killed all my energy."

He giggled. "Yeah, I feel the same." He paused. "You wanna sleep in my bedroom?"

I opened my mouth to reply when he interrupted me and pattered, "I mean, you can use it, and I'll just be here or sleep somewhere else!"

"Yeah? Can I sleep in your bedroom?"

He stood up, taking my hand to help me rise. Wrapping his arm around my shoulder, he walked me to the house. As we reached the door, it unexpectedly swung shut, and two guys stumbled out of it, laughing. They didn't pay any attention to us. I let them pass by before Raman gently urged me forward, guiding me into the darkness.

"Go forward. There will be some light soon."

I stepped carefully, and indeed, within a couple of seconds, I could see the light of his bedroom.

The room was completely silent. It seemed that everyone was outside now. We walked into the room, and Raman started knocking off the clothes on the bed and cleaning up the space for me.

"There's a key in the lock. You can shut the door so no one bothers you," he suggested.

I sank onto the bed. Everything started to blur. I felt the closeness of sleep, and my body was preparing to shut down.

"Can you lie with me for some time?" I asked.

"Um, yeah, of course." He kept standing there.

I lay back and smiled.

"Hey, you want me to lock the door?" Raman asked.

"Yeah, let's do it. You can open it when you leave."

I heard the key turning, and then I felt Raman's body settle heavily on the bed with his feet still on the floor. He let out a sigh.

I turned to face Raman, shifting up to rest my head on the pillow. We lay side by side in complete silence. My cheek touched the pillow, and my gaze was directed at his head, but I couldn't see his face, only the tip of his head. I was unsure if his eyes were open, staring at the ceiling, or if he had already passed out. I was afraid to move, fearful of ruining this fragile moment.

Suddenly, he turned to his side, facing my knees. He wrapped his arms around them, tucking his knees, and buried his face against my kneecaps.

"Hey…" I whispered gently, "What's up?"

He uttered dully, "I don't know… I'm just tired."

I ran my fingers through his hair and left my hand there, covering his head. He remained silent.

And there it all started—Raman, almost sobbing, began to share his story. He opened up about everything—his anxiety, his desire to run away, being sick of people, the feeling of being trapped, not getting fulfillment from NPL anymore, being surrounded by assholes, not being able to trust his friends... His entire life was unfolding beneath my fingertips.

"Will anyone even show up at my funeral?" he asked and looked up at me for the first time.

I ran my hand over his face and whispered softly, "I will come to your funeral."

He raised on his arms, bringing himself to my level. He stayed there, propped on his elbow, gazing at me for a few seconds before drawing closer and kissing me.

I hesitantly kissed him back, keeping it light, while anxiety churned within my chest. *Was this whole performance to just fuck me?* But I wanted to keep going. I wanted more of those kisses!

He pulled back, and when he looked at my face again, there was no hint of a smile. His eyes bore an unparalleled seriousness. Nervously, I let out a giggle.

Panic coursed through me. Raman wouldn't keep going without my consent, but I was so afraid. Afraid of what? Of being just one of his whores? Someone he'd forget about the next day? Someone he didn't respect?

Summoning my courage, I leaned forward and kissed him. He kissed me back and this time, pulled me closer to him. Raman tugged the hand he was wrapping me with underneath my body, and I was locked in his embrace. That turned me on even more. I didn't care about my fears anymore.

We continued kissing. I had no idea how long it was. At some point, he released my lips and lowered his head to plant a kiss on my shoulder. Then he leaned back and straightened his spine. I stayed in the same position, propped on my elbow, watching him. *What's next? Is that it?*

With a sigh, he gazed at the ceiling and said, "Look, I don't wanna fuck this up. Let's take things slow, huh?"

"Sounds good." I smiled and moved closer.

He turned his face to me and kissed me goodnight.

In a minute, he let out an annoyed sigh. "The light."

I grinned as he rose to switch off the light and then returned to wrap me in his arms once more.

O

When I opened my eyes, I found myself alone in bed. The room was bathed in the soft glow of the approaching dawn, with the first rays of sunlight gently infiltrating the space. The mellow notes of music played from the computer, filling the room with a serene ambiance. Faint voices carried from another corner of the house, their murmurs barely audible.

I propped myself up on my elbows, scanning the room. The ceiling was a muted shade of grey; the walls were painted a bright pink, and soundproofing panels adorned one of the walls. Did this room look the same last night?

I shifted into a seated position, tucking my feet beneath me and rubbing my eyes. "Fuck," I muttered aloud, realizing that my mascara had probably smeared around my face.

I climbed out of bed and made my way to the bathroom. The sand on the hallway floor clung to my bare feet, evoking a disgusted expression. I continued tiptoeing to avoid it.

The bathroom floor was filled with shampoo bottles, a dirty pink razor, and a forgotten towel. I looked at myself in the mirror. Well, better than I expected.

I turned on the tap and gargled. I cleaned up the rest of the mascara from my cheeks. Glancing at the towel on the floor, I opted for a piece of toilet paper to wipe my face.

The sounds outside grew louder, making it increasingly difficult to force myself to go there. I felt anxious.

I retraced my steps to the room, put on the shoes, snatched my jacket, and left the house.

Squinting my eyes against the rising sun, I walked in the direction of the voices. The fresh air was intoxicating, momentarily dizzying me.

I turned the corner and spotted a few people chilling under the sun. Raman was engaged in conversation with Miron and didn't notice me at first.

"Ooooh, our quiet baby is coming!" Miron laughed.

Raman looked over, caught sight of me, and smiled.

Miron continued mocking me, "Maybe at least in the morning you'll say a couple of words?"

Raman turned back to him with a serious tone, "Don't even dare to say anything to her."

"Oh-oh-oh! No comments about Raman's woman."

I smiled and took a seat on a windowsill beside Raman.

"You slept well?" he asked.

"Yeah, not too bad," I replied.

I didn't know what else to say. I didn't want to bring up last night in front of Miron, and I wasn't sure what else we could talk about.

Raman glanced at me, paused for a moment, and then shifted his focus elsewhere.

Meanwhile, Natasha and Pasha were fussing around, picking up their stuff. The anxiety about deciding whether to go or stay weighed heavily on my chest. I struggled to swallow the lump in my throat and took a few deep breaths to calm myself.

Natasha gestured, asking if I was joining them, and I responded with a shrug. I hopped off the windowsill and walked over to her.

"Natasha, I don't know what to do…"

"You really wanna stay here by yourself? With these people?"

I hesitated, struggling to find the right words. "I… I don't know… Something happened last night, and I feel like I should stay."

"Janina, don't let him make you one of his one-night stands."

"Natasha, I didn't sleep with him. It's not about sex."

"Well, you better know what it is about then," she said, stuffing her sweatshirt in the bag. "Let me know if you're going with us."

I found myself frozen in indecision, then let out a sigh. "I'm going home with you."

I scanned the room, searching for my bag. Once I found it, I looked at Raman, thinking about saying goodbye to him. He was busy speaking with someone else and didn't even notice I was getting ready to leave. I felt awkward and embarrassed to go there to him, Miron, Kraeva, and the rest. Suddenly, I felt like a complete outsider. I wasn't welcome there. So instead, I uttered a quick "Bye" and started making my way toward the stairs.

His voice called out from behind me, "Miazhevich, you're staying."

I halted for a moment and replied, "I have to go."

I smiled, hoping for a hug, a kiss, or at least something. Instead, he quickly turned away and acted like I had never existed.

O

Later that night, I found myself on a train, making my way back home. That was the end.

I couldn't bring myself back to normal life. I saw no point. I had an emotional burnout.

I couldn't understand what happened between us. It wasn't a joke. It was something, but it felt like this something had just died. Did I do something wrong?

Raman, trust me, I wanted to stay. I wanted it so bad... But I couldn't. I knew it would ruin my life.

> Bunny, how are you

Ian. Worrying. I could sense his anxiety.

< I'm normal

> Subnormal :)

Bunny, let's agree that you won't snort any shitty powders please

< I can't promise that

> I will end you :)

< Ian :)

> I'll seriously kill you if you keep doing that

< Do it

> Tell me what you're feeling right now

< I wanna fucking die

I didn't know what to answer. Ian was right. He was fucking right. I had been stupid enough to fall in love with someone like Raman. I needed to talk to someone, and I had no one except Natasha.

I hit send on the message and leaned back in my seat. It felt like the entire world hinged on her response.

Natasha's words were killing me. Especially how she liked to use this cheerful and funny tone when saying things that tore me apart. I hated myself for starting this conversation with her.

A few hours later, another message from her popped up on my phone.

> *Btw Pasha asked me yesterday if you had
> a crush on Raman*
>
> *I was like 'I don't know...' haha*
>
> *And he said that he hoped you understand
> what kind of person he is and that you
> can't have anything with him*

< *He said it to me as well when he was drunk*

< *I guess he doesn't remember that*

< *I said something about Raman and he said
> something like 'You understand that it's
> better not to hang out with him, right?'*

Natasha didn't answer anything. O*h, fuck you all! That's fucking bullshit.* It carried me away, and I texted Ian.

< *In case you were wondering, I haven't slept
> with Raman*

> *I don't even know what to say*

< *I just wanted you to know*

> *But you would want to?*
>
> *Since you're saying that*

Yes, of course. God, I wanted it so bad.

>

Well, it doesn't matter

You don't owe me anything

I've been feeling very shitty lately, such emptiness

I guess I need to start snorting drugs too

<

I feel shitty too.

Life is just a huge piece of shit :)

>

I don't want you to snort any powders, it's not cool at all

And it doesn't credit this Raman that he's doing it with you

I know too many people who just fucked up their lives because of drugs

It seems cool for the time being and everyone is so sure that shit happens to anyone but them

O

The following morning, I woke up, trying to remember the dream I had just had. Although I was physically awake, my mind was still entangled in the remnants of that dream.

In the dream, I found myself at a party with Stas, and an odd mission lay ahead—shopping for shoes for me. Weird, huh?

I navigated through the crowded room, gently pushing people aside in my quest to locate Raman. Back and forth I went, scanning the faces, but couldn't find him.

Then, I stumbled upon a door that led me into my father's bedroom. My dad sat at his desk, engrossed in something on the computer, with Raman lying on the couch right beside him. I tried to wake Raman up, pulling at him and crying out, "Raman, Raman, wake up!"

He stirred and said, "Janina, it wasn't for nothing. I swear it wasn't."

CHAPTER 17

August 2017

I sat in a bustling coffee shop, patiently waiting for Artsyom to arrive. Only a simple white wooden fence separated the space from the hustle and bustle of the nearby shopping mall. The noisy crowds passing by began to wear on my nerves, making me question my decision to meet here. But at least it was close to home.

I wasn't sure why I had suggested this meeting in the first place. While I was out of town, Artsyom mentioned a few times that we should plan a proper meeting to catch up, so it seemed I had no choice but to let him know when I'd be back in Miensk.

As I sipped my coffee, I observed the people around me. In the distance, I immediately recognized Artsyom's face towering over the crowd. He noticed me as well and flashed a grin. A mixture of annoyance and fondness welled up within me. I was indeed glad to see him after all this time.

He headed straight to the counter to place his order. By the time he reached my table, I had nearly finished my coffee, growing impatient for him to join me.

"Finally!" I exclaimed, rising from my seat to greet him with a hug.

"There you go," he said, hugging me back, "angry again…"

I rolled my eyes but couldn't help but smile.

"So, tell me everything," he said, sitting down. He raised his cup to his lips. "How's life abroad? Any new boyfriends?" He slyly smiled.

I returned his smile and started telling him everything: from my life since leaving Miensk to my friends, university, and all the general stuff, carefully sidestepping one topic that weighed heavily on my mind. I craved to open up about Raman and share my feelings, but I couldn't overcome the barrier, the distance between me and Artsyom.

"So, that's pretty much it about me," I concluded, shrugging. "How have you been doing? How's the baby?"

"It's okay, you know, normal life." He looked down at his cup, pondering.

"How have you been feeling?" I asked, and Artsyom raised his eyes on me. I quickly added to clarify my question, "I mean, your health."

"Uhm, it's good, I think." Artsyom took a sip of his coffee. "I have headaches sometimes, but other than that, I think it's all gone. I guess now you can call me a cancer survivor. *The* cancer survivor!"

"Nice, I'm really happy to hear it!"

The corners of his lips raised a little but his eyes remained calm.

"You sure it's all good?"

"Yeah… I actually should get going soon. You know, kids take all your time," he said with an awkward laugh as he reached for his jacket.

I hadn't expected the meeting to be so short.

"Uhm, sure!" I exclaimed a bit too loudly and hastily grabbed my jacket.

"Alright, Janina, I was really glad to see you," he said, leaning in for a hug.

"Me too. Will stay in touch?" I asked hesitantly.

"Yes, talk to you later."

As I watched his figure vanish into the crowd, I grabbed my bag and made my way outside.

The weather had taken a pleasant turn since the chilly morning, with the sun setting, and the fading light no longer bothered my eyes. I couldn't bring myself to face the crowds on public transport, so I decided to take a walk instead.

I held my jacket in my hands, feeling the evening's gentle breeze. The fresh evening air in late August.

The uneasiness I had felt about the meeting had dissipated, but it left me pondering why I had this strong need to share everything with Artsyom. How could he possibly help me?

I sighed, answering to myself that Artsyom would've probably been able to help me more than anyone else. He was the person who had faced death himself, when both of his parents died, but also when he was standing on the edge of dying from the tumor in his brain. Cancer, the life of an orphan, rejected by everyone, even his own relatives, not belonging to anyone or anything has maimed him so much that I was sure he would understand my pain more than anyone else.

I couldn't share my feelings with anyone. Of course, many people knew what was happening in my life, but if I told them how I felt, what would happen? What would they say to all my pain and wounds that will probably never heal? Nothing, that's right.

I pulled out my phone and texted Artsyom.

<

Wanna meet again sometime soon?

I waited for a few seconds, watching the three dots appear on the screen as he began to type.

>
How about Saturday?

O

>
I hope you'll drink whiskey with me

As I sat on the train on my way to our meeting, Artsyom's message came through. The excitement was rising in my throat, making it hard for me to hold back a smile. He was still there. The Artsyom I used to know so well was still there.

<

Uhm whiskey??

>
Yeah, I'm bringing a bottle

Plus some coke for you :)

<

Lol okay!

I was trying to nip in the bud all the excitement I felt about meeting Artsyom. It wasn't unusual for me to have these feelings, given our shared history. For a while, I had a crush on him while being in a relationship with someone else. After that relationship ended, Artsyom and I started dating but broke up just a few months later, after fighting almost every single day of our time together. Despite that, I still had an immense amount of love and care for him that didn't allow me to erase him from my life. Now, just a couple of years later, he was married and had a baby, so we kept a reasonable distance from each other.

The fact that Artsyom was bringing alcohol eased my nerves about the possibility of opening up to him. I desperately needed to regain that connection, feel that someone understood what I was going through and how much pain I'd been carrying in my chest in the last few months. I imagined crying on his shoulder, him wrapping me in his arms and telling me I would be okay. At some point, things would eventually work out.

I shook my head, trying to dispel the image. That scenario was simply not going to happen.

When I exited the train station, I spotted Artsyom already waiting, leaning against the railings near the entrance, engrossed in his phone, and gently clutching his backpack. He was wearing the same pink Vans slip-ons with Bugs Bunny as the day we met in the dog shelter. Now, the slip-ons were as faded and worn-out, as Artsyom himself. Nostalgia welled up in my chest, and my heart sank from sadness, missing those happy times.

"There she is!" He stood up after noticing me and giggled, "Drunkie."

"You're the one who brought the whiskey!" I snuggled up to him, wrapping my arms around him in a hug.

We made our way toward a nearby park, searching for a quiet spot to sit down. Along the way, we chitchatted about our days, work, people, and so on.

Then, I broached a somber subject. "My friend recently died."

It took him a few seconds to answer. "From what?"

"Overdose."

We kept walking in complete silence. We reached a meadow, and Artsyom pulled out a blanket. I nodded in approval and said, "Niiiiice."

He smiled and settled onto the blanket. Patting the spot beside him, he looked up at me. I eased down on the blanket and lay back.

"So, how do you feel about your friend?" he asked without looking at me.

I looked at his spine and the back of his head and answered, "You might actually know him. It's Raman. NPL."

"Ah, yeah, I've heard about that band." He leaned back and fell next to me. "So, how are you feeling?" he asked again, turning his face to mine.

"I don't know," I said, shifting my gaze to the sky, thinking about what to say. "I guess I'm okay?"

The truth was, I wasn't sure. I didn't feel pain anymore. I didn't feel anything inside. I enjoyed the wind tickling my nose, the warmth of the whiskey in my stomach, and the presence of Artsyom lying beside me. The topic was over.

"Seriously, I'm fine. Let's not talk about him anymore."

O

"INSANITY, INSANITY-E-E-E-E," I bellowed the NPL song into Artsyom's ear, grateful for the deserted streets of Uruchcha and the liberating embrace of Saturday night.

Artsyom chuckled, gently guiding me toward a bench as I continued to revel in my drunk antics.

Raising the nearly empty bottle of whiskey and coke to my lips, I pretended it was a microphone, launching into an impromptu rap session before collapsing into laughter at my own skills.

"You're not enjoying my singing, are you?" I whined.

"I enjoy your squeaking a lot!" Artsyom replied with a grin.

I playfully pulled my arm free from his grasp and tottered unsteadily toward the bench, each step a balancing act. Suddenly, the world hushed, leaving just the two of us on the bench, shrouded in silence. No cars passed, no trees whispered in the breeze, not even a breath could be heard.

"He is dead." I heard my brittle voice.

None of us moved. "I'm sorry."

Anxiety tightened its grip on my throat. I opened my mouth and exhaled, focusing on my breath, willing away the tears. I felt a burning sensation inside my nostrils. The air felt so fresh.

"I should've saved him," I muttered, hiding my face in my hands as I broke into tears.

"Janina, that's bullshit." Artsyom stood up without looking at me and pulled a pack of cigarettes out of his pocket. He slowly took out one and looked at me seriously. "You couldn't do anything. That was *his* choice."

"Artsyom, I could!" I pleaded, tears filling my eyes. "You… You just don't understand… All my life, I felt like I was missing something with him. Like, I should do something, but, for some reason, I just don't…" My voice cracked. "Even before he got into drugs, I was always leaving Mahilyow with this feeling. I knew I came into his life for a reason. I know this sounds stupid, but I should've done something."

He lit a cigarette and looked away for a second.

This fucking silence. It felt like for a moment, I stopped existing.

After taking just one drag, Artsyom tossed the cigarette to the ground and crushed it underfoot. He squatted in front of me, clasping my knees and looking into my eyes. Resting his chin on my lap, he let out a heavy sigh.

"Don't blame yourself. You couldn't do anything."

"I could have!" I exclaimed, tears streaming down my face.

He got up in anger. "What? Tell me, how could you help him?!"

"I could've been with him! I could've done something! Forced him to go to rehab, whether he liked it or not! God damn it! He would've been mad at me, he would've hated me, but he would've been alive!" I jumped up from the bench, seething with anger as I stared at him.

"You think it's so easy?" he suddenly shouted. "You really think if you wanted it, it would've just happened? Just like that?" He snapped his fingers. "You believe you would lock a drug addict in an apartment, and he would just be fine?" He laughed.

I retorted, "There are hospitals, doctors, therapists! I've watched so many videos and read so much stuff about different kinds of treatment…"

"So what? People go to rehab hundreds of times, then leave and keep doing the same!"

"He would've managed! Some hospitals even give guarantees for those who start using again and treat them for free."

"Jesus, you are so naïve! How do you think people die in hospitals? How do they get overdosed while being locked in? How do you think all this shit happens?" Artsyom stared at me in question.

I looked away from him.

"Everything is bought there. If a person wants something, they will get it. People die in rehabs every day! Get overdosed, commit suicide, or just go crazy, you know? Look, it's hard and painful, but you don't always have a solution. And with Raman, it was his choice. He was getting there, and he got what he wanted."

I raised my eyes to him, feeling completely hopeless, my tears already spent. I stared through him, the overwhelming desire to escape this pain consuming me.

Artsyom moved closer and pulled me against his chest. "Everything is going to be alright," he whispered into my ear.

I was so sick of hearing those words from everyone. The weight of it all became too much, and I couldn't hold back the tears any longer.

I clung to Artsyom, my sobs escaping, my face buried in his chest. It was the first time I had cried in front of someone since Raman's funeral. I couldn't keep the pain bottled up any longer. Christ, it was unbearable. I missed Raman so much.

While Artsyom held me close, I thought of how much I needed Raman. I closed my eyes and pictured him with me, wrapping me in his arms, my face nestled against his chest. Tears continued to trickle down my cheeks. I raised my face and looked into Artsyom's eyes. He looked at me and kissed me.

Suddenly, distant voices reached our ears, probably teenagers walking home from a party, chatting loudly and laughing. I glanced at a nearby bus stop and gestured toward it. Artsyom understood me without a word, retrieved his backpack from the bench, and moved ahead. I hoped the teenagers would continue and not stir up any trouble with us.

However, they didn't pass us by. The sound of their voices drew nearer and nearer. They were playing music on a phone, the bass thumping. One of them sprinted toward the bus stop where Artsyom and I now stood, the phone blaring the song. Before I could feel nervous, he approached me, shouting over the music, "Listen to this song! You surely know it!"

I couldn't understand what was happening or what he wanted me to listen to over the blaring music. I leaned closer to the phone, but it was too noisy to make out the lyrics. I asked him to turn it down and strained to listen.

When I heard the opening lines of the song, where the singer asked his friends not to mourn his death but to accept it and dance instead, I looked up at the guy in complete shock.

Of course, I knew it… It was the very song I had been listening to relentlessly since Raman's death. The song helped me get through this nightmare…

"Yes, I know this song." I smiled and felt the tears coming back.

"I knew that! It's the chorus now. Let's sing together!"

"Nah, it's sad. I don't want to…"

"Why sad? You should be happy!"

CHAPTER 18

June 2015–December 2015

I lay on the couch at my dad's house, absentmindedly scrolling through Facebook. The irregular hiss of the coffeemaker in the kitchen kept pulling me away from my thoughts. Annoyed, I stood up and closed the door. I needed to focus.

I lay back on the couch and continued to contemplate my options. I had to figure out what to do about Raman. Time was running out, and if I waited any longer, he'd probably forget about me. It had been four days since the party, and I knew he wouldn't text me this time. Shit.

I turned on my side, burying my face in the soft pillow in frustration. The velvety fabric caressed my skin. Shiiiiit… What could I possibly text him? I couldn't just send a "What's up?" because he would never answer something like that. I couldn't invite him for a coffee either. Why would he even want to have a coffee with someone like me?

A faint scratching noise caught my attention, and I turned my head toward the door. I saw a shadow underneath it, prompting me to get up and open the door.

"Thanks, kid," Dad said as he moved his feet away from the doorway.

He hurried to the table, placing the steaming cups on it before retreating to the kitchen for cookies. He always had cookies ready for me. His little daughter should always get her cookies along with the coffee. I could hear the familiar sound of him opening the large metal container and pulling out a bag of cookies.

"Do you remember that guy from the Rockets? He used to play the keyboard." I raised my voice to make sure he could hear me from the kitchen.

"Raman?" Dad asked as he entered the room.

"Yeah."

"I do! Why?"

"I've met him recently in Mahilyow. Hung out with him a couple of times." I reached for my coffee cup, and it clinked against the saucer.

"Yeah? That's nice. He seems like a good guy, huh?" Dad took a sip of his coffee and chuckled. "My girl always hangs with musicians! Funny, huh? I was the same."

He giggled once more and launched into a story about how he'd met members of his favorite bands. I spaced out for a second, after which I pulled back my phone and started typing.

<

Just told my dad I met you and he said he remembered you and that you're a good guy

haha

\>

Ahhhhha! Say a huge hi to him!

I appreciate that!

How are you doing?

<

Hahaha I'll forward him your kiss as well...

I'm alright

It's raining cats and dogs and I've just gotten
to my dad's place

On a bike lol

What's up with you?

>

By the lake with Mikola

Drinking to important stuff

Laughing at peasants

<

Say hi to Mikola

Why are you laughing at them?

Lol, poor peasants

>

Same for you!

Idk, rednecks are drinking here and it's so
much fun to watch

<

Lol I saw two drunk dudes today

"Why are you smiling?" my dad's voice broke my reverie, making me aware of the silly grin plastered on my face.

"What?" I replied, trying not to blush.

"I asked why you were smiling like that. What's up?"

I laughed. "Nothing. Just told Raman that you remembered him, and he asked me to say hi to you."

"Hi to him as well. So remember this old band called…"

I didn't listen anymore. Raman's messages had me on the verge of tears, overwhelmed by happiness. They were so warm. I felt like we were friends. Like he cared about me.

○

The morning after, I found myself seated at my office desk, typing on my computer. Suddenly, a subtle vibration from the phone resting on the table pulled my focus away. I glanced at the phone and froze.

Oh hi, mister Krasouski haha

*I'm working right now but I'll have a lunch
break in two hours*

You can come by and meet me here

>

Sure, send me the address

I set my phone aside and exhaled. SHIT. Shit. Shit. Shit.

I retrained my focus on the computer monitor, trying to pretend like nothing happened, but the text was floating before my eyes. This couldn't be real…

I reached for my phone, intending to text Natasha, but second-guessed myself. What would she tell me? Not to hang out with him?

With trembling hands, I poured myself a glass of water and gazed out the window.

The day was cloaked in gray, yet the sun fought valiantly to break through the clouds with slender, bright rays. I took a sip and thought, Whatever, we'll see what happens.

In the next moment, I found myself descending in the elevator, my heart racing uncontrollably. Ira stood beside me, animatedly gesturing with her long skinny arms, her words like muffled echoes in a bubble. It felt as if I were the one encased in a bubble, battling the madness within. Just a few more steps, and I would see him. Realizing that Raman was waiting for me right there, so close, was driving me nuts.

The elevator doors slid open, and we stepped into the sunlit hallway. The sunlight reflected blindingly on the wooden floors, making me squint.

Ira and I exited, and there he was, Raman, leaning on the

railing with a cigarette in hand, absorbed in his phone. Jesus, he was so beautiful.

He raised his head and smiled, noticing me.

"See you!" I sputtered to Ira and made my way toward Raman.

"Hey, Miazhevich!" he exclaimed, wrapping me in his arms. I couldn't help but think my coworkers would probably assume he was my boyfriend. I smiled at this thought. "Doing good?"

"Yes! So nice to see you!"

A big smile couldn't leave my face. I probably looked like a total idiot, but I couldn't help it. My entire being trembled inside, but I was trying hard to act normal. I couldn't fuck this up again.

I suddenly realized for the first time since meeting him that Raman had blue eyes. Walking alongside him, I turned to look at him again, to make sure I wasn't mistaken.

"What?" He chuckled.

"Nothing," I replied, struggling to suppress a smile, thinking that his eyes were indeed blue. How had I failed to notice it before? His eyes were so clear, so blue.

We decided to grab a coffee at Coffeebox and stroll around the neighborhood.

We delved into a myriad of topics during our conversation—life, politics, travel, his cat Chicka, music, my dad, work, and tons of random stuff. Every little thing sparked a passionate discussion. We didn't need to come up with ideas, new topics came up naturally, and we dove deep into them.

Time seemed to fly, and I wasn't ready to say goodbye to him. It's been almost an hour past the lunch break, but I didn't have enough courage to go back to reality and let go of his presence. Raman was worried I would get in trouble for being late, but I acted like it wasn't a big deal.

As we approached the office, the sinking feeling in my heart intensified. He hugged me, and when he stepped back, our eyes locked. For a brief moment, I thought he would kiss me.

Instead, Raman teased, laughing, "I'll send you that article later, and you'll see how fucking wrong you are!"

"You mean how right I am?" I grimaced. Somehow, I enjoyed being in a confrontation with him.

"Alright, Janina… I hope the rest of your day goes well. It was fun," he said with a smile and hugged me again. "I'll see you soon?"

"Uhm, yeah…" I mumbled into his ear, wrapped in his arms.

He let go and said, "Bye."

"Bye," I replied, watching him walk away.

I slowly walked inside, feeling confused. A part of me hurt and didn't want to believe he didn't kiss me again after that night. But another part of me felt confident. That other part of me knew that something big was growing between us.

Standing in the elevator, I impatiently waited to return to my office and text Natasha. My mind was a jumble of thoughts and feelings, my chest rising and falling rapidly, making me feel light-headed.

Upon entering the office, I offered Ira an apologetic look, and she responded with a reassuring smile, indicating that everything was fine. I hurried to my desk and quickly checked my screen to ensure no one had noticed my tardiness. Alright, all seemed good. I breathed out.

I grabbed my phone and sent a text to Natasha. I leaned back in my seat, thinking about what had just happened… Holy shit, this couldn't be true. I smiled.

A few minutes later, the phone vibrated. I opened the reply and held my breath.

> *Janina, I don't want to rain on your
parade, but as your friend, I don't want
you to fall into this trap. Despite what you
might be thinking right now, you should
remember that our precious and beloved
Raman doesn't believe in two things: love
and friendship. To him, all his friends are
just tools to gain benefits or profit. It's
all business. And girls who are peeing
themselves because of him are nothing
more than disposable bodies for one-night
stands haha*

> *So if it's about business, you have a chance
to stick around, but if you're a girl, you will
soon find yourself in his bed and then will
have to fuck off haha*

> *I'm not trying to hurt you. I'm just worried
about you. We all are.*

She was cruel. She always had this ability to hurt so much by acting all caring and loving. She knew how much I cared about him and spoke like this on purpose.

The phone screen lit up again.

> *By the way, he and Mikola are moving to
Saint Petersburg in September*

I put the phone down and held my breath. Raman was leaving.

O

For some time, I wondered why Raman didn't mention his plan to move to another country the day we met for coffee. Anyway, shortly after that, he indeed moved to Saint Petersburg. That was the moment when Raman's presence in my life stopped. I didn't try to reach out, and he stayed silent too. What was the point of trying if he wasn't there anymore?

O

As winter settled in, I realized I had finally moved on. I no longer sought updates on his life, and I assumed he wasn't curious about mine, either. But at the beginning of December, I got a notification on Facebook about an NPL concert coming up.

Without a second thought, I reached out to Raman, asking him to include me on the guest list since the tickets were already sold out. To my surprise, Raman was incredibly kind and did put me on the list.

In the days that followed, I felt like I was floating on air. I didn't know what to expect, but the prospect of seeing Raman again gave me goosebumps... Until the very day of the concert when I dared to ask him if it'd be possible to get in before the start to which he politely told me to fuck off.

On the day of the concert, I did my best not to let it get to me and focused on enjoying the show. It was still awesome that I got a chance to come for free, and I couldn't help but feel a sense of pride as I breezed past the line and entered with just my name. I felt special.

I didn't plan to text him. I was too proud. Instead, I was just out there, hoping he would pass by and see me.

Half an hour later, alcohol finally hit me, and I texted him.

Raman read my message right after the show but never replied.

CHAPTER 19

September 2017–October 2017

Life took a turn for the better after I moved to Sweden. The bustling streets of Stockholm welcomed me into a new chapter, teeming with unfamiliar experiences, social gatherings, and lively events. It all seemed to be working out so well, but for some reason, it only made me feel worse. I was constantly thinking about how insignificant all of this was compared to Raman.

The better my life became, the more often I caught myself thinking that I'd give it all away just to have him alive. Just to get a chance to wake up in the past, get scared by the horrible dream, and feel relief, realizing that Raman was alive. I was willing to go back to my senseless life in Miensk and continue getting disappointed, day after day, but to know that Raman wasn't gone.

My existence in Stockholm was an exhilarating whirlwind. The pace was relentless, each day bringing forth something awe-inspiring, yet as the city surged around me, my nights were haunted by persistent thoughts of Raman. I found solace, or perhaps a bittersweet refuge, in scrolling through our messages, his pictures on Instagram, and his Twitter posts.

Exactly two years before his death, Raman shared a quote from a song where the singer pleaded not to be saved from death, but from life instead. It made me wonder if Raman did feel better in the end. Maybe it really helped him?

Contemplating Raman's final years weighed heavily on my mind, a disquieting attempt to understand the depth of his struggles. I grappled with the notion that those years must have been arduous and empty, yet I knew I couldn't even imagine how painful they were. I just couldn't possibly grasp it in my mind.

I was reminiscing about his eyes the last time I saw him, trying to convince myself that nothing would've helped him at that point. Was there a reason to save him if, for him, it would mean just prolonging the pain? Maybe all these people who were smiling at his funeral were, in fact, the only people who knew him. The ones who accepted him and let him go. Including Nina. Did she understand him this well? Or maybe she was just too young to be able to force him to fight.

I hadn't done either.

CHAPTER 20

March 2016–November 2016

After receiving no response to my messages, I decided it was time to let go. I had a hard time keeping myself from someone who was obviously not good for me, but chasing someone who was clearly not interested was too much. I had more important things to care about.

Then, life took a dark turn when my father got sick, and I constantly blamed myself for not being able to help him. An ugly and nerve-wracking time of my life, when I felt like I was rotting from the inside while my dad was rotting from the outside.

The most unsettling revelation came later, at his cremation. Surprisingly, amidst the somber proceedings, I felt an unexpected sense of relief. As his casket vanished into the furnace, the burden on my shoulders seemed to lift. I straightened my back, bringing my shoulder blades closer together. I walked outside, inhaling the damp air.

Weeks passed, and just when I thought my heart muscle fully atrophied and I could never feel any emotions again, I met someone new. A Polish guy living in Norway who, I thought, would become my life partner until the end of time.

Nope. "Happily ever after" never happened. Our relationship crumbled a few months later, painfully concluding on a seven-hour bus ride. That sucked. What also sucked was my humiliating attempts to win him back just a few hours after he had left me for good. Following him back to Norway, trying to talk and solve problems because that's what adults do, isn't it?

What I got in return was complete silence. And no way to even pick up my shit from the guy's apartment. So, there was definitely no space in my head for our precious Raman.

Then, moving to Vilnius. This made my life feel a little better, which was strange, as Vilnius was not a place that usually made people feel better.

My mind suddenly brought a flashback of the wind furiously throwing raindrops into my face, snatching the umbrella from my hands. I shrugged from the memory and returned to my thoughts.

Maybe that shift in the environment still had some impact. Raman was becoming a distant memory, and I was immersed in living my life—until the holiday season beckoned, drawing me back to Mahilyow.

O

The screeching sound signaled the opening of the van door, letting in a blast of freezing air. In the dim light inside, Siargei's face barely registered, but the silhouette of his body melded with the darkness beyond the vehicle.

"Shut the door! They'll freeze!" Pasha shouted from the front seat, pointing at Natasha and me sitting in the back of the van.

Siargei squeezed his way in, closing the door behind him.

Attempting a smile, he stood awkwardly bent, head and back against the van ceiling.

"What's up?" Siargei asked, his strained expression making the attempt at cheerfulness look weird.

Not getting enough engagement from us in return, Siargei clumsily made his way to the front seat, starting a chat with Pasha.

Natasha and I were laughing, filming a video of our faces in a pale purple light, when I overheard Siargei whispering, "They both have pancreatitis. If not heroin, Raman would be alright but… he has one-two years left, no more."

Those words pierced through the music, reaching my ears even in the midst of the cacophony. *One or two years left. No more.* A sinking feeling enveloped my heart, and a wave of nausea overwhelmed me.

"Hold on," I murmured to Natasha, hastily exiting the car.

Two leaps later, I was retching onto the snow. Tears streamed down my cheeks, and my legs trembled.

The car door slammed shut, followed by hurried footsteps. Natasha and the guys rushed toward me.

"What's wrong? What happened?" Concern echoed from their voices.

"I'm alright." I halted my retching but still felt on the verge of doing it again. "Must have drunk too fast." I offered a feeble smile.

"Jesus… Baby, come here. I'll help you." Natasha wrapped her arm around my waist, assisting me back to the van.

Upon returning, an emptiness enveloped me. I felt detached, wanting to vanish and be alone for a moment.

The air was heavy with silence; no one knew what to say. Summoning courage, I took a deep breath and opened my mouth, unsure of what exactly I was going to say.

"Siargei," I paused, searching for words, "what were you saying about Raman earlier? Is he on drugs?"

"Uhm, yeah," he began, clearing his throat before asserting more definitively, "Yes, he is."

He was pronouncing every word so slowly, as though it pained him to even think of it. It felt as if he wrestled with the weight of each syllable, maybe aware of how much pain every single word was causing me.

That night, the harsh reality unfolded: Raman had been using heroin for a while. Several months in, four overdoses, one detox. The last time he overdosed, he got to a doctor who said that with pancreatitis, he had two years max. He had to quit if he wanted to live.

Shortly after that night, Raman posted a quote on Twitter about the relief from escaping the exhaustion and agony that comes with crossing to the other side of the world.

I wasn't sure if he wanted to live.

O

In the next few weeks, I navigated through a haze of pain. Walking around like a zombie, unable to talk, unable to feel, unable to think. Every action or thought made my stomach turn. I grappled with an inability to articulate my emotions, feeling lost in a sea of confusion.

As always, I tried my luck with Natasha.

<
I still don't believe Raman is doing it

Mikola - yes, maybe, but Raman - no

I don't know why but I know that

>
Who knows ☺

CHAPTER 21

May 2018

It was 4 in the morning, and I found myself meandering through the forest, trying to catch the night bus home. Not sure if deciding to walk alone at night in the forest was the smartest decision, but I was too high to continue partying. My mind was about to cross the line between reality and the drug abyss. Student parties were tricky, huh? Especially when you've been out of student life for ages.

Surprisingly, the forest wasn't scary. The crisp scent of the spring morning cleared my intoxicated mind. I was walking, carefully taking every step, trying to feel it to the fullest.

I stopped for a second, feeling a sudden warmth beside me. I held my breath in disbelief. Raman stood right next to me.

I couldn't see or hear him, but I knew he was there, looking at me. My heart filled with love, and my eyes were brimming with tears.

"Don't go…" I howled, my plea echoing through the quietude of the forest.

Beneath the first traces of light filtering through the trees, I stood still. Tears streamed down my cheeks, and a desperate refrain of "No, no, no… Don't go!" repeated in my mind.

Silence descended, punctuated only by my audible exhale cutting through the dense forest air.

He was gone.

◯

After the episode in the forest, the dam broke. I fell into an ongoing breakdown where I cried my eyes out every night until my body was fully exhausted from shuddering. The morning after, I'd wake up with a hoarse voice and get back to my normal reality. Until the evening would come, and I'd fall into the chasm again.

CHAPTER 22

March 2017–May 2017

Somehow, after returning to Vilnius, I managed to convince myself that Raman must be alright. It was all exaggerated, and he was definitely *not dying*. Come on. It was Raman. He couldn't just die.

With a renewed focus on managing my own life, I almost succeeded in pushing him out of my thoughts, aided by the fact that Natasha and I had minimal communication, leaving me on the outskirts of that particular circle.

My attention shifted to the prospect of spending the summer in Oslo. I secured an apartment, lined up a job, and was on the verge of packing when my ex from Oslo suddenly showed up again, adding an unexpected layer of excitement to my upcoming trip.

Life seemed to be falling back into place—until Natasha's April text shattered the tranquility.

>
Hiiiii, my girl! How are you?

*Do you know that you're supposed to be in
Mahilyow on the 21st of May?*

Can't break tradition, you know 😬

I knew exactly what she meant, but I wasn't sure what to answer.

The message caused a complete chaos in my mind. I couldn't drop everything and go there, but I didn't dare to miss a chance to see Raman. It had been so long since the last time I saw him. I felt everything shaking inside of me at the thought of talking to him. Just seeing him would have made my mind go wild.

I slept on these thoughts, and in the morning, I messaged the landlord in Oslo that I wasn't coming as planned.

A few days later, when my emotions went down, I texted Natasha.

<

About NPL...

*Even if I come, you should know that I'm
clean now*

I'm done with that shit

>

*Well, chances to have any kind of
party are super low in general*

Especially with drugs

Buuuut, never say never haha

So, we started planning the trip. And I started thinking about Raman more and more.

I knew something had changed in his life when I saw one of his interviews. He was seeing someone. When he was asked what kind of girl he wanted to fuck, Raman answered, "The one you're dating is the one you want to fuck." Someone who always mocked any kind of healthy relationship said something like that. On a show.

A bit later, I watched another show and it clicked. During the interview, Raman said hi to Nina. I didn't know who Nina was, but I knew she meant something to Raman.

I wasn't jealous, no. I just hoped Raman was doing alright. I hoped he had someone who cared about him and would get him out of this shit.

O

<

Ugh Natasha, my sobriety is fucked

I fucked up yesterday

>

How did you fuck up? Haha

<

I tried something that I really wanted to try

but never did

And I shouldn't have

>

Uhm?

<

Coke

>

Hahaha

How was it?

I pressed the send button and was instantly flooded with memories of the most harrowing comedown I had ever experienced after trying mephedrone at Raman's place. That feeling when the only thing you want to do is to walk out of the window. Ugh… But I missed mephedrone like crazy.

I stowed away my phone and redirected my gaze toward the window, greeted by an unappealing sight of the outdoors. The scenery, once vibrant, now wore a dismal façade.

Resting my chin on the plush back of the couch, I observed the world beyond the glass. Despite the sun's rays casting their glow, the grass and the trees were all dry. This disgusting yellow-brownish color. The grass looked dead.

I swiftly retrieved my phone once more, fingers trembling, as I typed a new message to Natasha.

O

As I packed my bags for Mahilyow, I realized that something in my mind had completely shifted. My future plans suddenly changed direction, and instead of the perfect plan for Oslo and the reunion with my ex, I saw Raman. Raman everywhere. I would wake up and have a coffee, thinking about him. I would later sit in a classroom, thinking about him again. I would then commute home on a bus, thinking about him. I was lost. I was obsessed.

All of this felt like a sign. As if the universe was giving me another chance to reconnect with him. There definitely was a reason for all of this.

My mind was going wild, anticipating the meeting.

O

Perched on Natasha's couch, I held a petite mirror in my hands, applying mascara with an unsteady grip. My hands trembled as my gaze nervously flitted toward the nearby phone.

I couldn't pinpoint exactly what I was anticipating. A text from Raman? But why would he text me? I wasn't sure. However, the lump of excitement bordering on anxiety was firmly sitting up in my throat.

Just as the screen illuminated, I hastily stashed the mirror and seized the phone.

> *You're sure you won't come to Oslo?*

I sighed, stowing the phone away. Strangely, the possibility of meeting with my ex, a desire that had consumed me just weeks ago, stopped touching my feelings. I had something bigger on my agenda.

The bathroom door squeaked, and Natasha came out, her eyes fixated on her own phone.

"Janina, Dzima is dead," she said, sinking onto the couch. Her gaze remained glued to the phone.

A wave of nausea rose within me. I didn't know who Dzima was, but the news seemed to suddenly cast a shadow over my entire future.

"Who is Dzima?" I asked, trying to cover my selfish thoughts with a look of genuine worry on my face.

"Raman's childhood friend," she uttered, and I held my breath, anxiously counting every second until she continued. "Pasha overheard at the bar that Dzima overdosed last night. He did drugs for the first time, fucked up, and died in his own vomit. Janina, this guy was not like that. He was a doctor." She covered her mouth with her hand, staring at me in shock. "Janina, what's going on?"

"Hey, calm down," I murmured, gently squeezing her shoulder to bring her back to reality. "Do you know exactly what happened?"

She reopened the message and started reading aloud.

"Dzima was visiting Raman in Saint Petersburg. They did drugs. Dzima choked on his own vomit and died. They're bringing his body to Mahilyow tomorrow. Don't say a word to anyone. This is a secret. No one knows," she recited, lifting her eyes to me, now brimming with anger. "Janina, it's Raman's fault!"

"Hey, calm down," I said again. "You don't know Dzima very well. You don't know what life he's been living. You have no idea what happened there."

Natasha opened her mouth to object, but I continued, "Neither does Pasha. Neither do I! Don't jump to conclusions after hearing some gossip."

I looked at her, hoping to see understanding, but her eyes were full of hate. She exhaled loudly, rose from the couch, and walked to the bathroom. She paused for a second before slamming the door, and then I stayed in silence. I felt anxious because the possibility of seeing Raman was rapidly going down to zero.

I realized I had been sitting there for a while when my phone vibrated, displaying Pasha' message.

> *Are you guys coming?*

> *Where are you?*

> *What's with Natasha's phone?*

< *What do you mean?*

I glanced at the time: 5:20 p.m. Nearly two hours had passed with me anchored to the same spot while Natasha locked herself in the bathroom.

> *Yo, everything alright?*

"Natasha?" I rose and approached the bathroom, my fluffy socks muting any noise, but an instinct urged me to maintain an even lower volume. "Natasha," I called out louder.

"Huh?" Her reply came without opening the door. Unsure if it was locked, I hesitated to invade her space. "Are you okay?"

"How okay do you think I am when you defend someone who is only harming people?" Her words were delivered quietly, yet each one seethed with intensity.

"Natasha, I'm sorry, but you don't know the full picture."

With a sudden swing, she flung the door open. Her gaze bore into mine, lips pursed. Her posture and face were dark, but the room behind her glowed in a yellow light. The silence thickened, becoming almost unbearable. I took a step back, allowing her to exit the bathroom. She followed suit, making her way to the kitchen.

I sighed audibly and sat back on the couch, facing her. Natasha appeared ostentatiously occupied, extracting dishes from the dishwasher and almost throwing them on the shelves.

"Natasha…"

She dramatically pivoted toward me, demanding, "WHAT?"

I opened my mouth, trying to find the right words, but nothing came out of it. My throat felt parched, so I closed my mouth and swallowed.

In a rush, she approached, a plate in one hand and a towel in the other, raising her index finger pointedly toward my face.

"Janina, I've told you a million times. He's a terrible person! Why can't you understand?"

I rose from my seat, gazing down at her, and spoke deliberately, "At. which. point. has. it. become. about. me?"

"It has always been about you! If you didn't try to hang out with him, he wouldn't even be in our lives anymore! And Dzima wouldn't…" She abruptly halted.

"Die? He wouldn't have died if I hadn't hung out with Raman? Are you fucking joking?" I dropped back onto the couch.

"I didn't mean that… I… I just can't lose people anymore, and with Raman, someone is always dying. It's never-ending… He's dragging people into this darkness. And you… You're just continuously trying to get into this darkness with him…"

"I'm not trying anything! I'm just enjoying spending time with him! I don't have a plan or anything. I know who he is!"

"Janina, I know you, and I see how you look at him. Even now, you dropped everything just to come here and see him."

Nervously grasping at the air, I searched for words, but nothing seemed to make sense. It suddenly dawned on me that I did drop the person I thought I loved, the city I wanted to live in, and my future plans, all for the tiniest chance of seeing Raman.

I covered my face with my palms and wept. Natasha sat beside me, wrapping her arms around my shoulders. I hugged her back, letting the pain pour out.

I cried and cried and cried. Natasha's shoulders were shaking too, but we didn't say a word anymore.

The doorbell rang, prompting us to release each other. Natasha offered a comforting smile, wiping tears from my cheek.

As she headed to the hallway, I tried to breathe and digest what had just happened.

Pasha burst into the room, exclaiming, "What the fuck! Why is no one answering messages!?"

He noticed my tear-stained face and turned to Natasha, who was following him into the room.

"What happened?"

Natasha answered, "Nothing. Just this crazy news made us break down a little."

Pasha turned to me again and asked Natasha while still looking at me, "Did she know Dzima?"

"Yes, a little," she fibbed.

"Are you guys still going to the concert? The cab is waiting—I couldn't drive myself."

Natasha glanced at me, waiting for my reaction.

I shrugged. "Yeah, we can go."

○

I stood, as always, at Pasha's bar counter, sipping my whiskey. Natasha lingered next to me, engaged in conversation with Pasha. My gaze fixed on the glass trembling in my hands, anticipation hung in the air. Raman was nearby, and I could feel his presence.

From behind the wall, the muffled resonance of Raman's voice reached my ears, sending shivers down my spine. The door to the chill-out room swung open, unleashing his laughter into the balcony bar space.

"Faggot!" he shouted into the room, his eyes scanning until they locked onto mine. "Heeeeey, you!" Raman rushed toward us, greeting me with a tight embrace. "Hello!"

"Hi," I managed to utter, my voice constrained by the force of his hold. Every inch of my body quivered as I felt his proximity, seeing his face again. This fucking charming asshole.

Releasing me, he grinned and declared, "Girls, you are way too beautiful to listen to Astap's music!" Then he burst into laughter again and left.

I remained rooted, numb, eyes wide open. When Makar passed by, saying "Hi," I couldn't even answer.

I was screwed.

A moment later, I exhaled and rested my head in my arms, leaning on the bar counter. Natasha placed her arm on my shoulder.

"Natasha, I'm fucked," I mumbled into the surface of the counter.

Pasha asked, "What's wrong with her?"

I lifted my head and reassured him that I was okay.

"Get up! Let's head to the couches," Pasha exclaimed. "Everyone's already there. Grab your drinks, and let's go."

I picked up my glass and followed the guys.

Approaching the couches, my anxiety skyrocketed. Everyone was there—Raman, Mikola, Siargei, some other guys, and a girl. I didn't know her and, in general, wasn't keen on seeing any girls around Raman.

I greeted everyone with a quick "hi" and slumped onto the couch in front of Raman.

"Hi! I'm Katsia!" The girl waved, her eyes scrutinizing me.

"Hi! Janina."

In the next few minutes, I heard the whole story of Katsia's visit to Mahilyow. Apparently, she was Siargei's girlfriend and a close friend of Mikola and Raman.

Discreetly glancing at Raman, I observed that he seemed okay on the surface. He was all goofy, playfully teasing Mikola. However, his excessive playfulness seemed out of place considering the death of his friend the night before.

Raman and Mikola started play-fighting like kids, laughing, and Raman intermittently shot me looks, as if this performance was meant to be watched. He was expecting a reaction. I forced a smile and looked the other way.

When they finished playing, I looked back at Raman and felt a lump in my throat. He was staring directly at me, his eyes devoid of life—an emptiness I could never forget. In that moment, I realized he was already dead inside.

"Raman, how are you?" I ventured.

"Fucking awesome," he answered, erupting into laughter—an unsettling, inadequate laughter. It made no sense to continue the conversation.

I found myself hoping he wasn't on drugs at that very moment. He couldn't possibly bring anything to Mahilyow. He had to be clean.

His laughter echoed again as he pointed in Katsia's direction. "Can you imagine, she was trying to save me!"

Katsia sat in the corner of the sofa, her expression dark. She stared back at him seriously, provoking even more laughter from Raman.

It hurt so bad seeing him acting like that. His eyes were empty. I wanted to hug him, take him somewhere safe. Save him.

Before anyone could say anything, Raman abruptly got up and left. Katsia started crying.

After we managed to calm her down and after a few glasses of whiskey, she began talking.

"He's just rotting inside!" Katsia suddenly turned to Mikola, unleashing her frustration. "You should save him! How can you not understand that?! You can't leave him alone like that!"

"Katsia, he is a fucking adult! He knows how to take care of himself!" Mikola retorted, not bothering to look at her.

She burst into tears again. She brought up Dzima's death, and I couldn't bear to hear it anymore.

Rising from my seat, I headed to the bathroom. Right at the entrance, I bumped into Raman. He was hiding something in his pocket. His eyes were glassy. He wasn't even seeing me when I was right in front of him. I was losing him. Right there, in the middle of a club hallway, I realized I was losing him forever.

I quickly used the bathroom and rushed back, hoping to see him there, but he was already gone.

A couple of minutes later, the raucous cheers of fans announced the beginning of the show.

I didn't even go down to the dance floor. Dejected, I walked to the other side of the balcony just to catch a glimpse of him. I didn't want to dance; I just wanted to look at his face a little longer.

He glanced at me once, scanning the space and pausing at my face briefly. The next time, his gaze intentionally sought mine, fixing on me for a while. From that point on, Raman didn't divert his eyes for more than a few seconds, repeatedly locking onto mine in the darkness of the balcony above the crowd.

It reminded me of that day two years ago when he formed a heart shape with his fingers. But now, it felt different. There was a resolute intent in his gaze—an intention to let me know there was something, and it wasn't lost. This connection eased my breathing but left me with a dull sense of inevitability. I couldn't quite grasp what exactly it meant back then, but it burdened my whole existence.

I observed him unabashedly. Maybe that confidence, the audacity with which I dared to meet his gaze, was what kept him looking. I didn't have this confidence the night we first met. He, too, looked at me differently. From the height of the balcony, I could sense how much he had changed. The person I once admired suddenly turned into a tired little boy. He was lost.

As the lights dimmed, I released my grip on the railing and sank into the couch. The cacophony of the crowd now felt distant as I embraced the silence. Tranquility nestled in the moment between the non-existent past and the yet-to-unfold future.

Gradually, my surroundings seeped back into my consciousness. People materialized beside me one by one, voices became audible, and I squinted against the flickering light from the bar.

The plan was to go to a bar, and I waited patiently for an update. Surely, there had to be a plan in place.

The guys went to the chill-out room to hang with the band and take pictures, but I didn't go. I was too shy. I was also confident I would see him later anyway.

Little did I know how wrong I was then, and how much I would come to regret it later. Why didn't I just join everyone? Why didn't I go to Raman? Just to be with him, hug him, look at him.

It was the last time I saw Raman alive. He didn't come to the bar.

O

The following morning, I awoke with a weight on my chest. A knot inside my chest was holding me so tightly I couldn't breathe or think. Anxiety was biting me piece by piece.

Rising from the mattress, I treaded carefully to the bathroom, mindful not to disturb the still-sleeping Natasha and Pasha. I grabbed yesterday's clothes along the way and softly closed the door behind me.

After getting ready and dressed, I gently opened the door to slip out when I noticed Natasha seated on her bed, absorbed in her phone.

"I was thinking about going for a walk," I whispered, and suddenly felt anger at my apologetic tone.

Natasha looked up and asked, "Can I go with you?"

That I didn't expect. "Uhm, yeah, sure."

Stepping aside, I let her use the bathroom and took out my phone, waiting for her to finish getting ready. In just a couple of minutes, she left a sticky note for Pasha, and we left.

For a while, we walked in silence. I knew we were both thinking about the same thing, but we probably never understood each other's perspective.

Unable to contain my thoughts any longer, I uttered, "I don't understand what to do." Natasha didn't immediately respond, prompting me to continue, "I can't just leave it like that with Raman."

"What do you mean?"

"He can die!"

"Janina, it's Raman. It's his life, and he's capable of making decisions for himself. You shouldn't get into this."

I exhaled heavily. "You know, I've always had this feeling... Every time I left Mahilyow, it felt like I should've done something, but I didn't. Like I'm missing something. So maybe now it's time to change that? It's just... When I imagine that he really can die... It scares the shit out of me..."

"I don't know, Janina... I think if you get involved, you won't change anything, but you'll only get into trouble. It's Raman. He's a rock star. He can't live differently."

"I don't know..."

This conversation started driving me insane. Natasha didn't hear me. She didn't even try. She couldn't understand a word I was saying. She knew Raman but treated him like a stranger.

O

The morning I was going to leave Mahilyow, I felt completely devastated. It felt as though someone had drained my soul and sapped all my strength from my body. An emptiness lingered within, leaving nothing behind. I was torn between not wanting to leave and feeling unable to stay any longer—a relentless urge to escape.

I was sitting on the couch, all ready, staring blankly at a fixed point in front of me. Natasha sat down next to me and wrapped her arm around me.

"Bunny, you look completely drained," she remarked, waiting for an answer, studying my face.

I remained frozen in the same position, fixated on the wall.

"Janina... You need to rest. You're just tired."

"I don't need anything. I'm sick of all of this."

O

As I traveled to Miensk, silent tears streamed down my face. Shielded by sunglasses, I allowed myself the solace of letting the tears flow freely without concern for other people on the bus. Occasionally, I lifted the sunglasses to wipe away tears when it felt like my eyes were overflowing with water, only to put them back on and continue my subdued sobbing.

It felt like it was the end. For the first time, I realized I might lose him forever any moment.

CHAPTER 23

December 2018

I arrived in Miensk just before Christmas, immersing myself in the city's festive atmosphere. The bustling streets were alive with the typical holiday buzz—crowds of people hurrying along the walkway between Kupalauskaja and Kastrychnickaja or waiting at the bus stop near the entrance to GUM, tightly grouped together as if it made them feel warmer. The only difference was that all of this didn't irritate me. I was smiling, looking at strangers, and they smiled back.

Returning home was a welcome relief. Well, this time, coming home finally did feel like coming home, in contrast to my usual feeling of obligation I experienced when having to visit my hometown regularly. I was excited to spend Christmas with my mom, visit Viera and her family on Christmas Day, and then go to Mahilyow for a quiet New Year's Eve celebration with Natasha and Pasha.

I missed Mahilyow. I had finally reached peace within myself and was ready to go there without the fear of breaking down. I also looked forward to visiting Raman's grave and spending time alone with him.

However, the plans didn't quite carry out that way. Exactly one day before the trip, as I was meticulously packing gifts into the suitcase, I received a message from Natasha asking me if I was okay with Siargei and Mikola joining the NYE party. The question was posed in a way that didn't leave me any room to say no.

Feigning enthusiasm, I replied with an affirmative "yes" but found myself sinking onto the bed as a wave of anxiety began to envelop me from within. Why did it have to be this way?

The burden of the loss was back on my shoulders, multiplied by the anxiety of the upcoming event.

O

On December 31st, I found myself in Mahilyow with the sole intention of spending as little time as possible with the group. We were going to be quite a big group in the end—14 people decided to join.

As I ascended the stairs within Natasha's building, a wave of nervousness washed over me, causing a persistent lump in my throat that made each breath a challenge. With each step, I found myself swallowing nervously, attempting to quell the rising discomfort in my chest.

I halted in the middle of the hallway, pressing my shoulder against the bright blue wall. The air carried a distinct dampness, a scent I had always loved. Amid the hushed surroundings, the steady thuds of my own heartbeat reverberated.

"Calm down," I urged myself, reminding that it was just a casual get-together, and I'd be heading home in just two days. With a reassuring exhale, I resumed my ascent up the stairs.

Reaching the fourth floor, I rang the bell, and the door swung open, bathing me in the golden glow of the setting sun.

Natasha greeted me with a warm hug, allowing me to step inside.

"You're alone?" I asked nervously.

"Yeah, Pasha went to pick up Siargei and Katsia. Are you hungry?"

Swallowing my apprehension, I replied, "No, I'm fine."

Natasha disappeared into the kitchen, returning with a red box adorned with a pink ribbon. Grinning from ear to ear, she handed it to me.

I approached, accepting the present with a shy smile. "What is it?"

"Open it!" Natasha chuckled.

Untying the ribbon and lifting the box's lid, I found a piece of fabric inside, initially offering little clue until I spotted Raman's last name on it. Perplexed, I opened my mouth in surprise, glancing at Natasha.

Impatiently awaiting my reaction, she nodded, encouraging me to proceed.

Extracting the fabric, I saw it was a t-shirt. The front showcased a cartoonish depiction of Raman in his classic stage pose, with the caption "I'm a legend." The back bore the name "Krasouski" at the top. I was speechless.

Staring at the shirt as if time stood still, I suddenly found myself overcome with emotion, tears streaming down my face.

"This is the best gift I've ever received in my entire life!" I exclaimed, my voice choked with tears.

Natasha drew closer, embracing me. "Come on, don't cry…"

"How?" I whimpered. "How did you get it?"

"Mikola sent them to us. Pasha and I got the same ones. We were so worried he'd mess up or forget, or that you'd stumble

upon these shirts online or something else would go wrong…”
Natasha laughed cheerfully.

“I didn’t see! I had no idea they were doing something like this! It’s Raman… Raman! It’s so beautiful! Thank you!” I still couldn’t believe my eyes. “Jeez, I love it!”

I put the shirt on and didn’t want to take it off. I just wanted to live in it and feel him close.

CHAPTER 24

May 2017–June 2017

Returning to Miensk unwrapped another layer of desolation within me. Sleep eluded me, and wakefulness felt like an impossible task. Exhaustion enveloped me, leaving me completely drained. The paradoxical yearning for nothingness conflicted with the urgency to act, especially as Raman's fate hung in the balance.

In this sea of uncertainty, my beacon of hope was Katsia. Determined to get at least some information, I decided to start with Natasha.

<

Are you in touch with Siargei's girlfriend?

The response didn't take long.

>

Nope

I stared at the screen, refusing to believe that was it. No elaboration, no breadcrumbs to follow.

Undeterred, I returned to scrolling through Instagram, trying to get distracted. Amidst all the noise, a horoscope post for my zodiac sign seized my attention. A particular phrase resonated, gluing me to the screen.

I reopened the chat with Natasha and started typing.

<

Can you imagine, I've just read in my horoscope that I shouldn't put all my effort into helping someone in a difficult situation if they got into this situation by their own choice

Otherwise, all further plans will be fucked

Btw my apartment in Oslo is confirmed

>

Wow

It hurt she didn't even try to understand me. Her brief and indifferent answers felt like tiny needles, each one puncturing my dying body.

<

Natasha, I don't wanna go anywhere

>

Baby, don't worry!

That was the extent of her engagement. That was all she had for me. *Don't worry.*

It seemed so easy for her to say these things. Even though she knew how much I craved her support, she wasn't there. She just stepped outside this problem as if Raman didn't exist in our lives at all. Strikingly, it wasn't just about Raman; it was about me. She didn't give a shit about the pain I was going through.

Luckily, I managed to find Katsia's contact details through Pasha. The only thing left was to decide how to start the conversation.

Taking a deep breath, I steeled myself and let the words spill out.

> *Katsia, hi! I wanted to talk to you regarding what you said about Raman. Can I do something or help in any way? It's just... my head is exploding from all of this. Always, since I met him, he was on something. He quit, then started again, then quit again... But now, it's just some insane shit happening. We need to get him out of it, but I don't understand what to do.*

My hands trembled as I typed this. It felt as though my entire world hinged on her response. If she didn't agree to help, I'd stay completely by myself in all of this. I had no more friends.

I was mad, particularly at Natasha. I wanted to fight with her and get some compassion. I needed some reaction from her. Any kind of reaction.

I messaged Natasha again.

> *I keep thinking about Raman*
>
> *Maybe now it's the moment when I should really take action?*
>
> *I want to help him in any way I can*

Even if it doesn't work, I'm not losing anything

It's just…

I can't go home and keep living my normal life after knowing it all

I won't take it if he dies

I don't give a fuck about others, about Mikola, NPL, Siargei…

Anyone but Raman

I texted Katsia, maybe she has ideas about what to do

I'm so lost

>

Janina, I don't know what to advise you

Really, talk to Katsia, maybe she'll be able to help you

You're both interested in it

And about you being tired…

Fuck, you really are tired, I can see it

I'm tired too but you're fucking exhausted

So do your thing and then just go and have some rest

What are you tired of, Natasha? Of ignoring the fact that your friend is dying?

I think I need to talk to Ignat again

I was on my way to Miensk, thinking about this stuff and I don't understand anything

I wanted so badly to go to Oslo and now, when everything seems to be working out, I got cheap tickets, the apartment is fine, slowly, things just become exactly the way I wanted them to but I still feel this despair

At the same time, I don't think that if I gave everything up and just moved to Mahilyow, I would be happy

I don't understand

It's just some dissonance going on in my head...

I need some enlightenment

You feel lost because you're tired, I think

Are you fucking joking? Stop saying I'm tired! I'm fucking tired of you not being there for me and Raman!

You just need to rest, relax and have a vacation

You need a really good rest, for your body and mind

I would also love to talk to Ignat about Raman

Ignat works with health issues, right?

I mean, people bring alcoholics and drug addicts to him, and he heals them?

I guess he should be pretty good with such stuff, idk

Maybe he'll advise something, who knows

Can you imagine how awesome it would be if I could bring Raman to him?

It's just that Ignat is such a weirdo and I feel like if Raman talked to him, maybe something would change

They grew up in the same place, maybe they even know each other

Yeah, agree

Maybe show him some pictures of Raman?

Not the old ones but something fresh

Maybe a picture will be enough for him to say something useful to you

And regarding bringing Raman to Ignat, this can be tricky

Remember how my coworker visited him and brought there her alcoholic husband?

She told me that the whole way this
dude was giggling, you know, laughing at
this whole idea of extrasensory perception
and stuff like that

The girl went first and her
husband should've followed

And before he even approached the house,
Ignat was like, 'You can tell him to go
away'

She asked, 'What do you mean?'

And he said, 'I can't help the one who
doesn't want to help himself'

She was fucking shocked

She didn't even manage to tell him a
single word about who that was but Ignat
had already understood everything and
given his answer

I'm not saying anything but if this works
out the way it should, I'll be very happy

I guess you'll be no less happy

<

I'd like to talk to him about stuff in general

About this feeling of incompleteness with
Raman, this whole situation

Ugh...

It'd be so awesome if they could talk to each other

Although, I know how unrealistic all of this is

>

I'm sure it's very realistic to get Raman to talk to Ignat

It's just that you need to build a connection with him

Not talking like 'I'm drinking, I'm eating, I'm shitting' but normal communication

He should want to communicate with you

Although, I have no idea if he's capable of communicating like that at all

No clue, to be honest

<

Well, you see how he talks to me, especially now

His communication is like 'I don't give a shit about you all'

But remember how it was before?

Even when we were in the trap house, he told me about so many things, asked questions

He asked me what I was doing in Miensk, what I was working with

I told him about dogs, about other stuff

He really has a brain and a normal attitude
toward the world

> *Well, everything that happened in the trap*
> *house...*
>
> *Take into account that it all happened two*
> *years ago*
>
> *And we were all a bit different two years*
> *ago...*
>
> *I guess...*

I stowed the phone and eased myself onto the bed. The sheets felt crisp and cool against my skin, casting a momentary spell of serenity and weightlessness. The tranquility, however, was short-lived as the phone stirred once more, and I saw Katsia's message.

> *I believe there's nothing we can do now. I*
> *tried, and everything I achieved was a block*
> *on Facebook and insults when meeting in*
> *person. Well, I'm trying to convince myself*
> *that everything is okay. But sometimes,*
> *when I get drunk, I try again to explain to*
> *others that we need to help Raman. But no*
> *one gives a fuck. As Siargei says, everyone*
> *just got sick of hassling around him. To*
> *which I answer that they're not really his*
> *friends then.*
>
> *My opinion is that now everything is so*
> *bad that we have only one option: put him*
> *in a hospital by force. But it won't help*

I was suddenly swept back to the moment when Natasha told me about Raman's childhood friend. It was hard to avoid hearing this story. Everyone knew about Dzima. A person who never did drugs, a doctor, someone who always helped Raman keep his head above water, gave in to Raman's persuasion, shot up with something, and died.

The memory flashed vividly before me, especially Raman's weirdness before the last concert. His empty look when he was on stage. He acted like he didn't give a shit, but he probably desperately needed to run away.

Katsia continued.

> >
>
> *The funniest thing is that Raman was the one who made his surrounding like that. But he needs a friend! Good, reliable, maybe even a chick who is always there, but not a stupid one. He needs to be excited about something. Something like what NPL used to be before.*
>
> *I sincerely regret going the wrong way with him. While we were friends, he was more or less afloat. He used to tell me shitty stories about the things he was worried about. We were just hanging out together, but then I started brainwashing him really badly, forcing him to go to AA groups, going myself to all these organizations and funds, and trying to find medications that would make him feel better. But everything ended up with a dialog:*
> *'Do I owe you something?'*
> *'No, I just want to help you.'*
> *'Fuck off, I don't need help.'*
> *'Raman, you're my friend. I'm worrying.'*
> *'I don't give a fuck. Go home.'*

*You should understand one thing: nothing
will work out until Raman wants it himself.
So many people tried to explain this to me,
a psychologist and a drug therapist, but I
did everything wrong.*

*Janina, keep me updated. I'm very glad
there are people who still care! It means
that Raman didn't blow all his friends.*

Friends... If only Katsia knew what kind of friend I was to
him. I was just a random person who was crazy in love with him.

The only thing that calmed me down a little was that even
though she tried to look like she accepted things as they were, she
was still hoping. In her every word, I saw hope that everything
would work out.

O

The following morning found me in the kitchen, quietly sipping
my coffee and thinking my plan through. The decision to make it
happen made me feel enthusiastic enough to push through with
it, despite the fears. This newfound determination also alleviated
some of the anxiety surrounding the ongoing situation with
Raman. But I needed a clear plan.

I knew I couldn't approach Raman just out of nowhere. It was
impossible to convince him of anything. Any abrupt action risked
being perceived as an accusation, guaranteeing his reluctance to
agree to anything. He was the smartest. He knew best.

Reflecting on potential influencers, my thoughts settled on
Ales from the Rockets. It struck me as odd that this idea hadn't
occurred to me sooner. Ales and Raman were pretty close friends.
Plus, Ales was older and, frankly speaking, smarter. Raman

would probably have much more respect for his opinions rather than mine.

I grabbed my phone and started typing.

<

Ales, hi

I wanted to talk to you about something important

Actually, first of all, I have a question

Are you in touch with Raman Krasouski?

>

Hi, Janina. :)

Well, I wouldn't call it staying in touch but we send each other birthday wishes.

Sometimes he invites me to concerts when he's in town.

That's basically it.

He texted me back so quickly that it made me even more anxious, realizing I needed to think fast.

Without hesitation, I tapped the voice recording button and began pouring out my thoughts.

I laid bare the severity of Raman's addiction, expressing my frustration with the indifference of his friends and their unwillingness to take any action. I complained about all the stupid excuses like "Well, he's always been addicted, and he knows what he's doing" and so on. I almost cried when I said I couldn't just leave him like that, that I needed help, advice, or any kind of support. My voice was shaking, but I didn't care. I knew how important it was to say that. I had nothing to lose except Raman.

Ales replied to my message right away with a short text.

>

*To be honest, I didn't know he was that
addicted.*

Injections? Heroin?

<

Yes

Both

>

Does he say so or it's actually true?

I was told that Raman had quit.

*Well, in general, you can't put your brain
in his head.*

*I love Raman very much but he's always
had this attitude toward drugs.*

He thinks that's cool.

*I hope he's strong enough not to get back
to it.*

<

He doesn't say anything

He just laughs and says bullshit

I saw him a couple days ago and...

Ughhh I don't know...

He looks bad, and I don't believe he quit

>

That marked the entirety of our conversation. After that, I felt an ugly feeling of pride in myself. Ales thought I was so caring and brave. Stupid selfishness. It satisfied my bruised ego.

But at the same time, I was so mad that he didn't offer any help. Nothing.

I needed to take action by myself, and I decided to try with Ignat. I knew it was usually hard to get an appointment with him, so I just texted him right away.

O

Surprisingly enough, only two days later, I found myself searching for a car to take me to Ignat. The night before, he had answered my message and told me to come.

I opened the messages again to make sure I got everything right.

> *Hey Ignat! I wanted to ask if you have any available time slots sometime soon?*

> *Yes tumorow*

> *Great, thank you! What time?*
>
> *Are you staying at the same address as last time?*

> *Yes janinna. you com seim adres laik last time. 11 in the mornin.*

> *Perfect, thank you so much!*

Anxious, I reached out to every car owner I knew, begging for help, with no result.

After two hours of fruitless attempts, I gave up and opted for a bus ticket to the town close to Ignat. His house was a little over seven miles away from the town, and I felt reasonably confident that I could walk the distance.

I hastily packed a backpack with only the essentials and made my way to the station.

The bus was stuffy, with a few open windows providing little relief against the scorching heat outside. Despite the discomfort, the prospect of walking seemed more appealing than enduring the suffocating odor of petrol.

As we approached the area, I walked to the bus driver, holding onto the seats, trying not to fall from the abrupt jumps of the bus.

The driver subtly nodded in response to my question, leaving me uncertain if he understood my ask. Luckily, he did stop at the exact spot I described and opened the door for me.

"Thank you," I muttered as I jumped off the bus stairs.

The bus quickly disappeared in the cloud of dust enveloping the surrounding like a fog. I pulled out the phone to check the route and started walking.

The scorching sun beat down relentlessly, causing my scalp to feel as though it were slowly melting. Even the water in my bag didn't taste as pleasant anymore as it was almost boiling hot. The sandals, abrasive and unforgiving, chafed against my feet. Yet, not for a moment did I question the decision that led me here. This, I knew, wasn't the hardest part of it all.

After enduring hours under the oppressive sun, the silhouette of Ignat's house appeared on the horizon. A sigh of relief escaped me as I quickened my pace.

In a moment, Ignat walked out to the porch and stood there looking at me.

"Where are you walking from?" he shouted, his blond hair ruffled as he scratched his head.

I waited until the distance between us was short enough for me not to have to scream and answered, "From the highway."

"You walked all the way from the highway?" he shouted again, this time in surprise. His ability to display whatever emotions he was feeling still caught me off-guard.

"I couldn't find a car."

"You're insane," he murmured. "Okay, come in."

Stepping aside, he ushered me into the house.

I've been there before, and the low ceiling, dense smell of aging, and weird Ignat's habits already felt familiar. He was a few years younger than me, but I trusted him wholeheartedly with my life choices.

Proceeding through the house, I entered a room with two armchairs facing each other. Glancing back at Ignat, I sat in the chair nearest to me after receiving a nod of approval.

The room fell into a profound silence, leaving me unsure whether Ignat still stood behind me. Eventually, the hushed footsteps resumed, punctuated by intermittent pauses and the faint sounds of items being moved on a nearby table. Uncertain if I should break the silence, I swallowed nervously.

Finally, Ignat settled into the chair opposite me.

"So, what's happening with him?"

"With whom?"

"With the guy you're trying to save." His blue eyes steadily looked into mine.

I gazed into his expectant face, taken aback by his grin, and began recounting my story.

O

Four hours elapsed before I found myself retracing my steps back to the highway, bound for home. A lump lodged in my throat, turning each breath into a torture. I couldn't cry or get angry. I just felt like it was the end. My last straw was sinking down, and despite how hard I was trying to hold it, it was all in vain.

My biggest mistake was probably telling Ignat right away that Raman was a drug addict. It made the outcome obvious to Ignat. Why didn't I just show him a picture of Raman and ask what he saw? Instead, I diagnosed Raman myself and only helped Ignat give up on him.

Most of my time there, Ignat responded to my story with nods and occasional remarks. His restless energy was distracting as he continually shifted in his armchair, trying to find a comfortable position by alternately stretching his legs toward the nearby table, tucking them under himself, or propping them up on the chair's back. He looked like a little boy, unsettled in his own grown-up body.

At the very end of the meeting, I started to cry, and he yelled at me. He got up from his chair and bent close to my face, pointing a finger right in front of my eyes, screaming that all of this was Raman's destiny and there was nothing for me to do about it. I screamed too, choking on my tears, that he didn't know what he was talking about. I was sure I could save him.

In response to my pleas for a meeting between them, Ignat coldly stated, "I can talk to him, but how will it help? He won't quit drugs until he wants it himself. There's just no sense in having that conversation." These words echoed relentlessly throughout the meeting, each repetition intensifying my refusal to accept this answer. I was raging.

At the same time, Ignat kept going with his rant and warned me that I would ruin my life if I got involved with it. "It will kill you," he cautioned.

A chill coursed through me as I recalled the most painful

revelation: "It will happen in August. It'd be good if someone could be with him."

I thought about the glimpse of hope I felt when he said it, the hope in my voice running out of my mouth, "I will be with him! I was going to visit him in August. I will!"

His response, delivered with quiet indifference, echoed relentlessly in my mind. "Don't get false hopes. You won't save him."

Playing this dialog in my head was unbearable, prompting me to reach out to Natasha for solace.

As soon as she picked up the phone, I hastily began recounting every detail of what had happened.

"He can't help me with Raman. He told me that Raman had totally given up on himself.

"He said that yes, he worked with drug addicts before, but those were easy ones, weed, and stuff like that. While here, he said, that's it. His exact words were, 'I don't see any future for him. You know that yourself, he won't die old.'

"He told me that Raman would be alone when it happens. I tried to get any information, and every time, he was like, 'It's not your destiny, don't do anything.'

"Also, he seems to know about those several half-deaths. He said everything will happen in August, and it'd be good if someone could be with Raman then."

Natasha stayed silent during my whole speech and only quietly added afterward, "I agree with everything he said. You want to help someone who doesn't need it. It's nothing more than your wish, which is just a waste of time and effort. I guess that was his main point?"

"His point was that Raman will die, and I won't change anything."

CHAPTER 25

December 2018

As we approached the cabin we rented for our New Year's Eve celebration, anxiety gripped me, promising me a night that would be anything but enjoyable. I walked into the cabin with my head sunk into my shoulders, scared to raise my eyes.

When we walked in, Katsia came to me first and wrapped me in her arms. Then the rest joined us in the hallway, and the space filled with quiet chatter.

A few minutes later, we were already drinking, blasting music, and laughing. Seated on a bench by the table, I watched the lively scene. Pasha circulated through the crowd, giving away belated Christmas gifts. Natasha stood in the corner, whispering something to Alesia.

Mikola burst into the room, holding a bunch of absurd sauna hats in his hands. His infectious laughter soared above the music as he handed out hats to Siargei and Pasha. They gave him an "Are you an idiot?" look, but obeyed. They started making weird moves, mocking old men in a sauna, still unable to talk because of the non-stop laughter. I couldn't help but giggle too.

Katsia walked into the room, rolling her eyes at the playful antics. Siargei tried to wrap her in a hug, but she deftly pulled away from his embrace, making her way to the table and settling into the seat beside me with a sigh.

"Beware of kids in the room!" she exclaimed cheerfully, popping open her beer.

"Yeah," I answered, contemplating my next words.

Strangely, her presence didn't feel weird to me. Instead, she was giving me a feeling of a safe place. I felt more at ease sitting next to her than I did with the rest of the group, including Natasha. Maybe because Katsia was the only one in whom I hadn't gotten disappointed.

The party continued with even more alcohol, music, and laughter. No one mentioned Raman, and I slowly stopped thinking about him myself.

The beer wasn't enough anymore, so I reached for a bottle of whiskey, preparing to mix it with coke, when Katsia suggested, "Wanna go outside to smoke?"

"Oh, thanks. I don't smoke," I replied, appreciating the offer nonetheless.

"We can just chat," she shrugged, extracting a cigarette from the box. "It's getting too noisy in here."

"Okay." I grabbed my glass and the whiskey bottle, trailing after her. It was indeed becoming too loud in the room, and I wasn't catching up with the fun going on there.

Outside, the air was crisp and cool. It got suddenly so quiet. The only audible sound was the distant hum of the party, as we strolled toward the wooden gazebo. From there, the clamor of the celebration seemed miles away.

Taking a seat on the bench, I added a splash of whiskey to my glass and sipped it as Katsia abruptly uttered, "I hate Mikola. So much."

"What?"

"You heard me. He doesn't give a fuck. Not about Raman, Alesia, or anyone else. He only thinks about himself!"

"Well, that's Mikola," I responded with a nonchalant shrug.

We sat in silence for a brief moment, after which Katsia spoke again. "I know what was going on with you and him," she disclosed, the sudden change of topic catching me off-guard.

"What do you mean?"

"I mean Raman. Mikola told me."

She paused, anticipating my response, but I remained silent, lost and confused.

"A year or two ago, when they were both drunk, Raman told Mikola about you. How he was afraid to move things forward between you two. I mean, because of how different you two were. He was scared of messing things up, you know? You were a good girl from a good family, and he was a fucking junkie."

She chuckled, calling him a junkie, and looked at me. I couldn't crack a smile, and neither could I say a word. My tongue felt numb. She continued.

"When you offered help, I thought you two were just friends, you know... I had no idea you had a history together."

I could barely hold back the tears. One more word and I would break down.

I opened my mouth, but the door flung open, and the loud company barged out.

The air felt invigorating, but my thoughts were clouded. I didn't register the voices of the people emerging around us. I was sinking and didn't even try to swim.

Suddenly, Alesia gripped my shoulder, and reality snapped back into focus.

"She always does it!" she exclaimed, still gripping my shoulder. "She starts talking to someone, and then they're both gone for hours!" Her laughter echoed as she leaned down, wrapping her drunken arm around my shoulder.

The serene place Katsia and I were in just a moment ago was now filled with drunk laughter. I glanced at Katsia; she met my gaze, pursing her lips in disappointment.

For the rest of the night, I drowned myself in alcohol, seeking solace in its numbing embrace to stifle the ceaseless thoughts swirling in my head. *Stop, please, stop! I can't!*

With unsteady legs, I stood up, wearing a forced smile.

"It worked!" I exclaimed.

Natasha looked at me in surprise.

"It worked!" I repeated, trying to take a few steps. However, my legs betrayed me, and after only two stumbling strides, I clutched a tree branch, trying to maintain my balance. I burst into laughter.

"Alright, I think we can call it a night," Natasha suggested, walking over and looping her arm around my waist. With her support, I navigated back to the house and up the stairs.

A fire already crackled in the fireplace, casting a warm and cozy glow across the room. The dimmed light was pleasant to look at. The pain seemed to be gone, and so did my ability to speak.

I sank onto the couch, curling up my knees. Natasha covered me with a blanket and settled on the floor beside me.

We stayed there in silence, and I felt so at ease until the painful thoughts found their way back. Why isn't Raman here? What would it be like if he'd made it until now? Would we be celebrating New Year's Eve together? Would I curl up in bed next to him? Would he wrap his arms around me and kiss me goodnight?

CHAPTER 26

June 2017

I was sitting in Manufaktura, sipping my coffee and waiting for Viera. There was something about their coffee that made me feel at home. The place was filled with people and the subtle buzzing of chatter.

Spotting Viera, my heart leaped with joy. She could always bring out the best feelings in me, give me hope, and cheer me up. She pointed at the queue, meaning that she was going to order her coffee first.

After she was done, Viera sat on the couch next to me and gave me a hug. After the usual "how are you" chatter, I couldn't help but speak about Raman.

"Remember when we sat here, talking about Raman after I first met him? How crazy it all felt to me and how sure I was that he would never text me!" I chuckled at my naivety, or perhaps at my luck.

Viera joined in the laughter, and the moment felt serene, carefree, and effortless. Viera started telling me something else, but I was deep in my thoughts. I suddenly felt so empowered. I got this hope that made me feel like everything would eventually work out. It couldn't be otherwise. This mood gave me some unusual energy to try harder, look for options, and get back this lost connection with Raman. Possible actions were already gathering on a list in my head.

"You should just text him and offer to meet up!" Viera stared at me in question. "Are you listening?"

"Um, no! I can't do that!" I felt a blush creeping up my cheeks.

"Come on! You have nothing to lose! Jesus, you're so afraid of rejection!"

"It's not about rejection. It's just... What if he doesn't even reply? What do I do then?"

"Well, if he doesn't reply, whatever! Not the end of the world..."

I sighed. Viera had a point. Things couldn't get worse than they already were.

Deciding not to waste a moment while I felt brave enough to do that, I immediately texted him.

<

By any chance, are you going to Miensk anytime soon?

I'm here until the end of the week and would be happy to meet ☺

It sucks that I see you only at concerts

I set my phone aside, determined to resist the urge to check for his reply every second. Yet, as soon as Viera and I bid each other farewell, I gave up and opened the chat. Read. Ugh.

Later that night, I woke up to the sound of a message. I propped myself up on my elbows and reached for the phone.

> *Raman OD'ed*

> *He's alive*

I read Katsia's message again and sank back onto the pillow. *Alive.*

I thought for a second about this whole situation and felt embarrassed for myself. I, such a fool, wrote him lovely messages while he was lying on the bathroom floor, completely out of it. *Overdosed.* I silently sobbed.

Ping. A new message.

> *Mikola moved out*

These words struck a sense of panic in me. If even Mikola was leaving, it meant that everything was falling apart. Raman was now alone in the apartment. If he overdosed again, there would be no one to help.

Feeling compelled to share about my visit to Ignat, I decided to spill everything to Katsia. I told her every detail, from Ignat's opinion on our efforts to save Raman, to his thoughts on Raman's future and his mention of August.

I asked Katsia if it made sense for me to visit Raman in August and stay with him for some time.

> *Of course, he'll surely be down for you visiting*

> *I'm not sure I believe all this stuff about August, but having you there, keeping an eye on him, is actually a great idea*

The prospect of seeing Raman in a couple of months brought relief, but soon after, fear and panic gripped me. I had no clue how to handle it if he decided to shoot up. Would I be in danger?

The rest of the night I spent engulfed by anxiety. Was this all too much to handle? Did I get involved with something I could never manage?

Suddenly, the words of both Natasha and Ignat, warning me about the potential of ruining my life by sacrificing everything for Raman, started making sense. But there was no way back. Not at this point.

O

The next morning, I reached out to Natasha to tell her about the overdose. Her response was terse.

> *I guess everything is coming to an end. His Kurt Cobain games have to end at some point.*

O

The next few weeks I spent in some sort of loop. I'd wake up early morning, rush to check messages and make sure Raman had been online, and then fall back asleep until the afternoon. Then I'd get back to my *normal* business of watching YouTube videos and scouring articles about how to save a drug addict, what to do in case of overdose, how to talk to them, and so on. Then I'd start over the search for clinics and professionals and, as always, end up with one or two options of those that seemed adequate enough.

Then, when it was late enough for me to force my body to bed, I'd spend hours, unable to sleep, staring at the ceiling, thinking about whether he was alive.

Eventually, I'd manage an hour or two of sleep, only to awaken in a panic and check my phone. If Raman was online, I could fall back asleep. If not, I'd stay awake for hours, praying for him to be alive.

I would wake up the morning after, and the same thing would happen again. It was an endless loop, and I couldn't continue living this way. I needed to do something. I needed to talk to Raman.

I wrote a note on my phone with a message I wanted to send him. It was very open, way too straightforward for me, but I knew I had to do it. He deserved to know how I felt about him. I clung to a small hope that it'd move something in his mind.

Later that day, over coffee, I shared the note with Viera and asked her what she thought.

She quickly ran through the text, handed the phone back to me, and raised her eyes in surprise.

"It's so personal…"

"I know… I'm just scared, you know? He can die any moment, and I'll never forgive myself if I don't tell him how I feel about him."

"Well, I'm not a good advisor here. I'm sorry… But you know best what you have to do."

Yes, I knew exactly what I had to do. I copied the text and sent it to Raman.

<

I remember how I met you when I was 14. I was so damn shocked by how talented and smart you were. How much you loved music

I went offline immediately after sending it, but shortly after, I realized I couldn't just sit and wait, so I opened the message to see if he had seen it. He did. *Read*.

That night, for the first time in a while, I was falling asleep calmly. He knew everything. And he knew he wasn't alone.

CHAPTER 27

January 2019

The day after New Year's Eve found five of us tightly packed in a car, heading toward the cemetery. Siargei and Pasha occupied the front seats, while Natasha, Katsia, and I squeezed into the back.

The awkwardness was definitely on our side of the car as the guys were chatting as usual, while I wasn't sure how to break the silence at the back. I didn't know how to react to what Katsia shared with me the night before, and of course, I didn't mention it to Natasha. So, we collectively opted for silence, pretending to be engrossed in the music.

As soon as we drove over to the parking lot, I recognized the place. I was quite delusional on the day of the funeral, but surprisingly enough, I remembered everything too well.

Exiting the car, I looked at the surroundings, recalling the day I spotted Nina there when she whispered a quiet "hi" to me. My mind replayed the path to the graveyard, following the group bearing Raman's coffin. I remembered how I couldn't get my eyes off him, couldn't get enough of his face, and couldn't bring myself to say goodbye to him. How painful it was to stop looking because I knew I would never see him again.

While the guys were preoccupied organizing things in the car, I strolled toward the cemetery. I wasn't sure if I remembered exactly where the grave was, but a walk in the forest would do no harm to me.

The path ended, revealing chaotic rows of graves. Big and small gravestones with photographs of people. Subconsciously, I started calculating the years between their birth and death. 73, 49, 68, 6. Jesus… The images of people buried there were flashing in front of my eyes. Until I saw Raman's grave.

There was no gravestone yet, just a hill of soil and a metallic cross with a sheet of paper with Raman's photograph. Tons of flowers covered the hill and spread around the grave. Mostly, chamomile. *His flowers.*

Seating myself on a wooden bench by the grave, I looked at his picture. Suddenly, I felt at ease. The anxiety that had clung to me for months seemed to be finally gone. I could breathe freely, the weight on my chest lifting.

It felt so weird to realize that Raman was there. He hadn't disappeared. He was right by my side. So close.

CHAPTER 28

June 2017–July 2017

I stood by the window, an empty cup in my hand, my gaze fixed on the somber gray sky. The coffee maker emitted a comforting hiss and whistle, immediately diverting my restless thoughts. Turning away, I seized the pot, filling my cup with the steaming coffee. I added a dash of milk and wandered back to my room.

Dim light filtered through the matte glass door of my mom's bedroom, casting a gentle glow in the hallway. The morning was hushed, the only audible sound being the muffled thud of my footsteps.

As I tried to discreetly close my room door, the soft creak of my mom's door opening caught my attention.

"Already up?" she asked.

"Yeah, can't sleep anymore. Figured I better do something more productive than studying the ceiling," I replied.

"You're okay?"

"Yeah, of course," I forced a smile long enough to make her believe that my only concern was a lack of sleep. "Alright, I'll go read something. See you later."

Closing the door, I released a breath I hadn't realized I was holding. It took me some time to gather the courage to open the browser and begin researching clinics.

With each tab opened came a sip of coffee, a glance out the window, contemplation about the cost, a fleeting search for hope, and the final gulp of coffee. My mind teetered on the edge of overload. It didn't seem realistic. The plan just didn't look like it had any chance.

Most of the clinics looked like total scams. Some seemed more or less okay but cost a ton of money. But what worried me the most was not the money but bringing Raman there. How in the world would I convince him to agree to that?

My phone vibrated with new messages from Katsia.

> Hey, what if we ask Raman's dad to help?

> I mean, he can't say no to us trying to save his stupid son

Closing the laptop, I grabbed my phone and settled into bed. It did sound like a good idea, but I couldn't imagine texting him. Too much guilt on my shoulders to ever be able to look Raman's dad in the eyes.

< Can you get us his phone number?

> Yes, sure, I'll text Miron. Hold on

Restlessness overcame me, prompting me to pace the room, twirling the phone in my hands. Eventually, I perched on the bed, burying my face in my palms.

The phone buzzed, and a message displaying the coveted phone number illuminated the screen.

I stopped breathing for a moment. The help could be just a message away. But what if Raman's dad had no idea about his son's addiction? What if it would only make things worse?

My mind spiraled, conjuring a myriad of potential scenarios and their outcomes. The only certainty was the need for action.

I didn't trust Katsia's ability to show empathy and decided to text Raman's dad myself.

Before my fingers could touch the phone again, the screen lit up with new messages from Katsia.

>

Miron said that Raman is planning to quit

Miron is willing to help

Alright, no time to think. I hastily typed the first words that surfaced in my mind and clicked send.

Hours later, after countless laps around the room, a response finally appeared on my screen.

>

Hello. I don't know who you are and
what you're talking about. But silence is
consent.

Perplexed, I stared at the screen, unsure what that was supposed to mean.

I sent the screenshot to Katsia. She replied right away.

>

Well, what else could we expect?

Siargei said he wasn't surprised

*Raman's parents don't give a shit about
him*

<

But what should I answer?

Insist on a meeting in person?

>

Yeah

Mention Siargei

They've known him since he was a kid

Within the next 20 minutes, it was all settled. I was meeting
Zmicier in four days, and there was no turning back.

As the outside world plunged into darkness, my anxiety
swelled. I had no idea what to tell him. I had never had a normal
conversation with him, and I wasn't that close of a friend to
Raman. This whole idea suddenly seemed terrible. Why did we
need to get parents involved?

I grabbed my phone and typed a message to Natasha.

<

I feel so anxious about Oslo

It's driving me crazy

I haven't felt like this for ages

>

Anxious about the job?

<

No, the job didn't work out

I'll babysit next week

The other family bailed at the last moment

But maybe that's even better

At the end of June I'll probably need to come back

We decided to put Raman in a clinic

Don't tell anyone, it's a secret!

I just have this feeling that everything is wrong

I don't want to go to Oslo but I don't know what I want either

It's just this stupid apathy

I'll probably stay in Oslo for a week or something, have some rest and come back

>

In a clinic??? How?

Someone said he'd been there and it didn't
help!

<

I found a few clinics that look reliable

They all do this intervention thing

Long story short, it's when family or friends, along with a doctor, therapist,

245

or another specialist, visit the addict and convince them to go to a clinic

I don't know how it all goes

I need to call them and ask

But the important thing is that they don't use force, they just convince

Although, we need to decide together with his parents

Katsia got their contact details and I'm meeting Zmicier, his dad, on Monday

Also, Mikola came to Raman again and told him that if he doesn't quit, he will lose everything and Raman promised he'd seek help

And I think that in this situation, we have pretty good chances...

I can see that he wants to quit

That's why I feel like he will agree

Anyway, will see what his parents say about this whole idea

>

And his parents, I guess, know that Raman is fond of such stuff?

<

Yes, they do

Look, it's been so many years of him being on drugs

\>

Uhm, okay. I hope it works

○

The next four days unfolded in a strange apathy. My body hurt. I slammed onto the bottom. I couldn't fall any lower but couldn't rise either.

I found solace in the confines of home, rarely venturing outside, fixated on my laptop screen, fixing stuff for Oslo. My flight was in five days, and regardless of how I felt about it, I still needed to find an apartment, a job, and finally, start packing.

On Sunday night, I couldn't sleep. The upcoming meeting with Zmicier on Monday and the flight to Oslo on Tuesday kept me short of breath. My heart raced, an incessant rhythm echoing in the silence of the night.

I got out of bed and made a few push-ups to get my body busy with something other than thinking. Out of breath, I lay back down in bed, trying my best to feel tired and to muster even the slightest desire to sleep, but nope, nothing. The flow of thoughts immediately returned, leaving me lying wide awake. What if Zmicier tells me to fuck off? What if he's so rude I won't be able to even ask him for help? The what-ifs were driving me crazy. 02:57 a.m. Ugh, kill me.

By 04:47 a.m., the alarm was set to ring in just two hours, yet I was already wide awake, anxiously counting down the minutes.

I couldn't find a comfortable position to fall back asleep, so I quietly got out of bed, careful not to wake my mom, washed my face, got dressed, grabbed the keys, and left. Before closing the door, I glanced at the glass door leading to my mom's room. For a moment, I felt the urge to talk to her, tell her everything, and ask for help and support, but I shut myself up and closed the door.

I hailed a cab from the street, and two minutes later, I was already on my way to the bus station. I opened the app to change my booking for an earlier bus, and luckily, there were seats available. 5 in the morning isn't a peak travel time, after all.

Upon settling into my bus seat, fatigue washed over me like a heavy wave. My body felt soft and heavy.

As I closed my eyes, anticipating a good nap, a barrage of anxious thoughts flooded my mind. How should I start the conversation with Zmicier? How much does he know? How will he react? The thoughts were chasing one another. My brain refused to shut down.

Angrily, I opened my eyes and breathed heavily. The few passengers on the bus engaged in muted conversations, a gentle murmur filling the air. A stifled giggle, a child recounting a kindergarten tale to his mother, and two elderly ladies discussing a new hospital in Mahilyow created a backdrop of ordinary life.

I looked out of the window. The never-ending bright yellow fields, with the sun starting to rise above the horizon.

My heart sank when I imagined what would happen if Raman actually died. Tears filled my eyes, and I briskly wiped them away with my hand.

"Calm down," I quietly pronounced out loud.

○

Arriving in Mahilyow, it was still the crack of dawn, leaving me with at least a couple of hours to kill before meeting Zmicier.

I got off the bus by the department store and immediately felt like I was home. The bustling street, teeming with people, exuded an air of anticipation. The morning heat only started coming up from the asphalt, but the air was still fresh.

My steps led me toward the Slavy Square. The idea of chilling on the grass with the view over the river and the suburbs spreading for miles ahead was tempting. In the midst of uncertainty, this city had consistently been a wellspring of hope and support, and I desperately needed to fill the void.

Passing by the Cuba club, my heart sank with pain. The whole story of me and Raman started there. Memories flooded back to the day we first met, standing before the stage, captivated by his performance and enchanted by his tattoos. How much had happened since then. I've aged so much during this last year.

A few moments later, I found myself tugging at the weighty door of "Buffet" to snag a cup of coffee. The place wore an eerie emptiness, yet the servers scurried about in a hushed frenzy, creating an atmosphere of subdued chaos.

"Mornin'! What can I get you?" The question snapped me out of my thoughts.

"Uh, just a latte," I murmured in response.

Perching on a soft red couch, I waited for my coffee. I looked over my shoulder to see the seats where I was sitting with Natasha and Pasha the day after I met Raman.

The door slammed, sending a shiver down my spine, dreading the possibility of running into someone I knew. I couldn't bring myself to tell anyone the real reason for my visit. Relief washed over me—false alarm.

My attention shifted to the counter, where the server wore a welcoming smile as she handed over my cup. Rising to my feet, I reciprocated the smile, grabbed my coffee, and left.

As the first sip touched my lips, I savored it for a moment, feeling the weight on my chest lift. Warm air brushed against my skin in tandem with a cool morning breeze.

I walked to the Slavy Square and settled on the grass behind the monument. The flags above me rustled with a distinctive pop. Glancing at their tips, I chuckled at their nervous dance in the wind. I was still in Mahilyow, and things were going to be fine. I knew that.

Just as I started to enjoy the moment, my phone vibrated. I clicked the button to answer it.

"Hello, Janina. It's Mr. Krasouski."

"Hello," I replied, my voice hushed.

"I'm finishing sooner than I expected, so if you're free, we could meet at 11 in the park? The one on Piershamajskaja Street, close to Cuba. Do you know how to get there?"

"Yes, I'll be there."

"See you then."

He hung up before I said goodbye. My stomach churned. Suddenly came the realization of what was going to happen. I panicked.

Rising from my spot, phone trembling in my hands, I headed toward the park. Coming closer, I noticed how busy it was with all the kids running around. Summer vacation. They were cheerfully playing and laughing, and I was dying inside.

I peered into the faces and saw Zmicier. I recognized him right away. Not even by his face, but by his posture. A tired man stood there on a path, staring into nothing. I wanted to cry and hug him.

Approaching Zmicier, I cleared my throat, and he raised his eyes at me.

"Hello, Mr. Krasouski. I'm Janina." His face lit up with a warm smile, so sincere that my heart sank.

"Hello, Janina! So glad to finally meet you. Texting is not the same, you know? We need more human connections, just like that."

I extended my hand for a shake, but he took a step forward and wrapped me in his arms instead.

"It warms my heart to know that people like you care about Raman. Thank you for that."

I hugged him back and felt like I could barely hold my tears. I saw *him*. I saw Raman in the face of his father and felt his warmth in Zmicier's embrace.

"You're all shivering. Do you want to sit here?" He gestured to a nearby bench, and we silently made our way there.

"Zmicier, to be honest, I don't know where to start. You probably already know that Raman was... is... on drugs. And now, it got really bad. He is..." My voice quivered, and I grappled with how to proceed. "He is on heroin now."

Zmicier's gaze remained fixed, staring ahead without uttering a word. His face retained its kindness and openness, but I could see how much he struggled with words. Unsure whether to continue or let him digest the news, I hesitated.

After a long pause, he whispered, "Are you sure about heroin?"

I looked at him with immense sorrow.

Still looking at the ground, he continued, "I mean, he has tried different things, but it was just experimenting. You know, teenagers like trying new things. I don't think he would ever get to the point of trying heroin. He's a smart boy. You know that, right?"

"I do, of course. He is smart. But unfortunately, this is true. He's on heroin, and his state is pretty bad."

I halted, almost delving into how close Raman was to the grave, when I noticed Zmicier's transparent eyes, filled with hope, staring at me. I couldn't bring myself to ruin it.

I continued, "We have to help him. I have some ideas on how to get him back to normal life. I found some hospi..."

"We could probably manage without a clinic! Raman is not a junkie. He can manage!"

"I'm sorry to say, but now it's too late. We need to take action right now, or..."

"I know, I know! But what if he faces problems afterward? He'll never get a normal job! What if they take him to court?"

"They won't if we do it in Saint Petersburg. And Zmicier, whatever happens, Raman will be alive. That's what we should care about."

Zmicier let out a strange chuckle, opened his mouth to speak, but ended up exhaling instead. He dropped his head into his hands and sighed. "Okay, what's your plan?"

"There's an option called intervention. You, as a parent, sign an agreement with a clinic. Together, family, friends, and a therapist from the clinic go to Raman, convincing him to get help. They know how to talk to such people…"

"Such people? He's not a piece of trash!"

"I know, Zmicier! All I mean is that they are experts! They work with people struggling with the disease Raman has. Miron is willing to use the tour cash for this, so no need to worry about money."

"These programs are for people with no choice. Raman, thank God, is not among them. I'm sure about it! He needs to stay in a normal drug dispensary for some time and get rid of the substance abuse. Please, team up with Miron and Mikola. They're Raman's best friends. They know what to do."

"Of course, Zmicier. Miron and I will talk to clinic representatives and try to arrange something right after the tour. We can't waste any more time."

He nodded and dropped his head into his hands again. I sat there, looking at Zmicier, pondering how fragile even a strong adult man can sometimes be. How hopeless.

The silence from Zmicier made me think that the meeting had come to an end.

"I'll keep you updated," I said quietly, placing my hand on his shoulder.

He reciprocated by placing his hand on top of mine and squeezing it. After that, I stood up and walked away.

Once a safe distance from the park, I called Katsia and told her everything.

"Was that really everything you talked about?" she asked.

"Yes! The entire meeting lasted like 10 minutes. He was really upset and shattered..."

"Well, not shattered enough, apparently, since he won't agree to fucking shut Raman in a clinic!"

"Listen, it was all new to him. I can understand. He's super afraid it'll affect Raman's future."

"Isn't he afraid that his son won't have a future?"

"I know, Katsia, I told him the same." I could hear the frustration in her breath through the phone. "At least he agreed to detox."

"What's the point? Raman will leave the clinic, hang out with his junkie friends, and shoot up again!"

"Look, we can start by convincing him to do detox and then try to push further. Miron and Mikola are on our side. Maybe they'll talk to Zmicier too. He trusts them."

"That's fucking bullshit. What kind of father is he...?"

I sighed. We stayed on the line for a little longer, discussing the details of the plan. After that, I walked back to the bus station.

O

Later that night, I saw Raman in my dreams. It was one of those vivid dreams where you can't quite tell if it's reality or not.

In this dream, Raman and I were dancing in some kind of hangar, surrounded by many people. But I danced only with him. We were looking at each other, hugging and laughing. I felt an overwhelming sense of happiness and tranquility. But then I noticed how people around were looking at us—with disapproval and condemnation.

I glanced at Raman, and he said, "You shouldn't be dancing with me. They look this way because they know it'll break you. If you keep dancing with me, you'll ruin your life."

Without saying anything, I leaned against him and continued dancing.

O

The next morning, still caught in the remnants of a strange dream-induced haze, I reached out to Natasha with a text.

<

I'm worrying about Ignat's words regarding Raman

About August

I'm pretty sure Raman is clean now

I have a feeling that he did quit

But the longer he stays clean, the more dangerous it'll be if he fucks up

What if he holds on until August and then does it again?

It'll surely be an overdose...

>

I don't know, Janina

It's not your headache at all

<

I just can't continue living as if nothing is
happening

>

You can't change it either

It hurt. It hurt so badly to know that no one was supporting me in my attempts to save Raman. No one cared. Except for Katsia. She was the only person with whom I could actually talk. She understood me better than anyone else. But even conversations with her became more and more hopeless.

Lying in bed, wrestling with the elusive embrace of sleep—my nightly ritual for the past few months—I received a text from Katsia.

>

Looks like Miron is trying to bail

I got a sick feeling in the pit of my stomach.

>

He's just texted me that it'd be better to
stop such active participation in this

He says Raman knows what he has to do

I asked him if he understood that it's too
late to leave it up to Raman to which he
replied that Raman has connections among
experts and we don't need to get involved

255

                                                     <

                                               Oh, shit

                             Do you think Miron really means it?

>

Means what?

                                                     <

                     His belief that Raman will take action
                                               himself

>

I mean... I don't know

                                                     <

                          Fuck... We should've expected it

                     I knew Miron would bitch out once he
                     realized that it's just a new burden on his
                                              shoulders

>

I'll try to push more

                                                     <

                     Do you think we could manage with just
                                       having Mikola?

                     Would it be enough to convince Raman?

>

The thing is that if Miron bails, Mikola will
follow him

They are both fucking sick of taking care
of Raman

I was already typing a message to Zmicier, describing in detail what an asshole Miron was to quit right now.

Almost immediately after clicking the send button, I got an answer back.

Speechless.

I took a screenshot of the message and sent it to Katsia.

*And if even his dad believes that
everything is ok, we aren't able to prove
anything*

You know what the funniest part is?

*His dad knows everything about overdoses,
alcoholism, addictions. And he gives zero
fucks about it*

Lol what a joke

Mikola was online, and I sent the same screenshot to him. I didn't want to believe that it was going to end like that. No fucking way.

The preview of his message back killed the rest of my hope.

\>
Janina...

Look, it's too much right now

*He's not that bad to make such decisions
for himself*

*Let's do that if everything goes out of
control*

Now he's managing, he's trying

Everything is ok for now

\<

For now... Cool

\>
Seriously, I'll take him to the clinic

I found myself at a loss for words in response to these messages. It was as if all my energy had just evaporated, leaving me feeling weak and indifferent to everything.

○

The next couple of weeks I spent collecting unanswered calls and messages. The notification badges on app icons on my phone grew one by one, but I couldn't bring myself to write anyone back.

Shortly after the lost fight with Mikola, Zmicier, and the rest, I left Miensk and headed to Oslo.

The city greeted me with its rainy and cold embrace. I was enjoying the time of peace, the fresh air of Oslo, the weird eclectic (and expensive as fuck) apartment in Majorstuen I was renting, and the feeling of reconnecting with my old self once again.

I could finally breathe, spending days walking around or perched in a chair by the big window. I would make pasta with vegetables and bring the plate to the same armchair to eat, watching the rare passers-by outside. I felt at ease, even though I knew this was temporary, and soon enough, a new flow of anxiety would land on my shoulders.

During one such tranquil evening, curled up in the armchair with a glass of iced coffee, the screen of my phone lit up.

I reached for the windowsill to grab the phone and saw Raman's message.

>

I'm alright. Don't worry about me 🤍

Immediately sitting upright, I brought the phone closer to my eyes. What?

I opened the message but didn't know what to answer. My heart pounded in my chest.

I couldn't figure out what to answer even the next morning. Neither did I a few days later. I left Raman hanging there, but I knew he was doing well, and I didn't need anything more.

It indeed seemed like things had started working out when I got a message from Katsia.

>

Good news. Raman is in the hospital

Detox and laser cleaning of arteries

*He gets out in a week, finishes the tour
and then goes to rehab*

In the fall we'll find out if there's any result

<

Oi, that's amazing!

Do you know if he went there by himself?

*He texted me last week saying he was all
good and that I shouldn't worry*

>

Of course not by himself

Mikola kicked the shit out of him

He yelled at him and threatened him

260

I was so happy to hear the news and see some progress that I couldn't help but text Raman.

So how are you? How's everything?

\>

Cut my neck.

He sent a selfie—lying on a hospital bed with a tube protruding from his neck. Dark circles clung to the undersides of his eyes, but a faint smile graced his tired face. God, how much I've missed this man.

\>

What about you, kid?

I'm in Oslo. My home 🤍

\>

I want to come to Oslo too

Oslo is wonderful

\>

I need to see you

I mean, I wanted to talk to you

Sure

I'll come back in a few weeks or you can come here if you want to

\>

I do!

I sank back into my chair and looked out the window. I wanted to cry. Happiness was tearing me apart. The prospect of everything falling into place felt like a gentle tremor coursing through my body. Just a little more time, and everything would be back to normal.

O

Before finishing the message, tears welled up, and I hit send. She read it right away.

I found myself staring at my phone, constantly touching the screen to prevent it from locking even for a moment.

A few minutes later, the screen lit up with a reply from her.

> *Wow... I'm shocked.*
>
> *Janina, I don't know what to say...*
>
> *As your friend, I am strongly against you starting any kind of relationship with a person like him. Common sense plays the most important role in me, and it says that you don't fucking need this. But if I look at it from a more humane point of view, all these factors... Shit, you really are in love with him. It's obvious. And if I weren't your friend, maybe I would say that you should try. But in reality, I can't think like a stranger, and I want you to have a worthy guy by your side. Not Raman, unfortunately. So, of course, I won't support any actions from your side toward him.*

I messaged her back right away, trying to explain myself and tell her more about how I felt, to which I never got an answer back. Not a single word.

CHAPTER 29

July 2019

"You sure you don't want me to go with you?" Derek's question hung in the air, unanswered for a moment.

"Yeah," I mumbled, without looking at him. I reached for the seatbelt's buckle, my fingers fumbling slightly with the familiar mechanism. "I want to go alone."

"Okie-dokie," Derek enunciated as he slowly turned the steering wheel and glanced into the rear-view mirror, skillfully maneuvering the car into the parking spot.

A twinge of guilt pricked at me for not giving Derek a warmer answer. He was so calm and understanding of everything. He went with me all the way from Sweden to Belarus to meet my family and friends and to just get to know my homeland. And he drove me to Mahilyow, to this very spot in the middle of a residential neighborhood filled with gray, dirty, high-rise buildings. A spot by the lowland where I once met my *friend* Raman.

In the months since Derek and I had started dating, he had once asked about Raman, questioning whether there had been more to our relationship than just friendship. "Uhm, he was just a friend," I answered back then.

I remembered the nervous gulp that caught in my throat, noticing for the first time the identical dimple on Derek's chin, mirroring Raman's. Derek's arms were also covered with tattoos. Too much to handle.

As we finally parked, Derek's calm yet puzzled expression turned toward me, and I couldn't resist but smile.

"It's just a place I used to hang out at," I said, my voice unexpectedly coming out in an overly-positive and high pitch.

"Then why don't you let me go with you?" He raised his arms off the steering wheel and then placed them on his lap.

I gently placed my hand on his cheek and said quietly, "I want to be there alone for some time. Please, let me have that."

"Fine." He sighed, but I could sense he was okay.

I quickly patted my pocket to ensure my phone was there before turning to Derek for a kiss. He gave me a gentle peck on the lips before I opened the door and stepped out of the car.

Though it was mid-July, the sky was cloaked in gray, casting an ominous hue over the surroundings. Following the path away from the parking lot, I glimpsed the edge of the lowland where Raman used to live.

As I drew nearer, a pang of nostalgia tugged at my heart. I looked down and saw the bonfire pit, surrounded by a few wooden benches.

Glancing to the left, I scanned the lowland for any signs of life and realized that the house was gone, replaced by an excavation site. Piles of soil loomed next to the excavator, with stacks of cement bags nearby.

For a fleeting moment, doubt crept in, tempting me to go back to the safety of the car, to my fiancé, and to the familiarity of my normal life. But I brushed away those thoughts and gripped the wooden railing of the stairs leading down.

The wood felt cold, damp, and yielding beneath my touch. I carefully stepped on the stair, making sure it could hold me. Then took another step and then another one, taking me closer to the bottom.

As I descended to the ground, I glanced back up at the beginning of the stairs and felt a shiver run down my spine. "Well, I'm already here. I can just have a quick look and head back up," I reasoned with myself as I made my way toward the benches.

Pausing once more, I gazed at the vacant space where the house once stood. Memories flooded back—the porch illuminated by a solitary lamp, surrounded by darkness. I remembered us on the porch, heading inside, with me at the front and Raman following behind, his hands on my shoulders.

In my mind's eye, I saw us all bustling into the house, laden with bags of food and drinks, trying to hide from the unexpected snow, our laughter ringing out joyfully. Giant snowflakes danced in the air at the end of April, swirling and twirling in the warm glow of the lamp above the door. The murmur of laughter and chatting echoed from behind the closed door, once we were all safely inside, enveloped in warmth and dryness. Outside, the yellow flickering light from the windows painted shifting shadows on the now snow-covered ground.

As I observed the heaps of soil and the looming presence of the excavator, it suddenly dawned on me that the lowland was being buried. Scanning my surroundings, I comprehended the stark reality—there were no other buildings around anymore, only rare trees, their branches brittle and weathered, and the metallic basin that once cradled flames, alongside the now-deserted benches where we used to gather.

I walked toward one of the benches and sat down. I couldn't bear to raise my eyes to the fire pit or the vacant space where the house once stood. Instead, I fixed my eyes on the ground, consumed by my desolation. What had happened to me? To my life?

I wanted to cry but tears wouldn't come out. I frowned my eyebrows so hard, wanting the pain to just come out of my body but it didn't help. I clenched my eyes shut, and a solitary tear trickled down my cheek. Focusing on the bench before me, memories flooded my mind—Raman's powerful bass and his thunderous laugh reverberating through the air. I could almost see a dance of the birthmarks on his face when his lips stretched in a smile, the flicker of flames in his eyes.

I suddenly wanted it all to disappear. Derek with our perfect life, the years spent in Stockholm—everything. More than anything, I wanted to turn up at this same spot, that night, before I lost Raman forever.

"Please, please, please," I begged aloud, consumed by quiet despair, tears streaming down my cheeks as the biting chill of the air nipped at my skin.

I pleaded for just a glimpse of his face, a fleeting moment to hear his voice, a chance to look into his eyes once more, bury my face against his chest, and hide in his embrace.

Muffling my sobs with trembling hands, I looked around through a curtain of tears. It was all gone. My entire life, everything that had been important to me, was now gone forever. And I had disappeared alongside, leaving nothing behind but an empty shell of who I once was.

O

I stood at the top of the stairs, frozen. Though I knew I had to return to Derek, I found myself unable to move. I wanted to look back, to etch the image of the bonfire and the handful of benches into my memory. I wanted to remember the laughter that once echoed in the warmth of the night on that first day of summer. I wanted to erase August from my memory and stay in the months when Raman was still with me.

Glancing over my shoulder, I watched as darkness began to swallow the space below. With a heavy heart, I pushed aside the pain and made my way back to the car.

Quickly wiping away my tears, I drew in a deep breath before opening the door. As I sank into the seat, a damp chill seeped into the car.

"You good?" Derek's voice broke through the silence as he turned the key in the ignition.

"Yeah," I replied softly, avoiding his gaze as I stared out the window.

We then slowly rolled forward, through the hazy streets of my second hometown.

CHAPTER 30

August 2017

"In the dream, everything happened in an apartment with a very expensive interior. Everything was mirrored—floors, ceilings, furniture. The floor was paved with big square tiles forming a way forward. There was something like sand on the tiles. As if someone spilled something there, you know? I stepped on the tiles and walked to the bathroom. There, I saw Raman lying in the bathtub. Naked. He noticed me and tried to get up. He wanted to leave, but I was stopping him for some reason. He looked so weird. I don't know how to explain it. He was alive but seemed dead.

"The next moment, I saw him in the corridor of the same apartment. He was wearing a tracksuit, that kind of navy old-school tracksuit. He looked as if he was going to leave. I said, 'Wait! Where are you going? I'll bring you the phone. Hold on.' He hugged me and said, 'Baby, I'm okay.'

"I left for another room to grab the phone. I remember I couldn't find it for a while and then suddenly noticed it in a pile of clothes in the corner of the room. The phone also looked weird. You know, these old phones with buttons? I took it and rushed back to the corridor, but Raman was gone. I ran to the other room to look out the window. It was high. It felt like the sixth or seventh floor. I saw the trees but couldn't see him and realized he was gone."

CHAPTER 31

June 2015

I open my eyes. A gray ceiling, the room painted in bright pink, with soundproofing material covering one of the walls. The distant hum of music filters through the room from a concealed speaker.

Propelling myself up on my elbows, I try to peer through the window, only to be met by an impenetrable darkness veiling the motionless trees outside. What time is it now?

I fumble beneath the pillow in search of my phone. Ugh, where is it? I suddenly feel nauseous and let my head fall back onto the pillow. Something is wrong. Something bad has happened.

I hear some chatter outside. Men's voices.

I make another attempt to sit up. My feet find the floor, and I cautiously test my ability to stand. Nausea doesn't come back, and I slowly rise.

I feel weird about going outside to these people whose voices I can't even recognize, but I see no other choice.

On my way to the exit, I pass by the bathroom and stop for a moment. Plastic shampoo bottles are lying around. I notice a dirty pink razor in the corner and have to swallow the nauseous lump in my throat. I turn around and continue my way to the door.

I don't understand what's going on. Of course, I recognize this place, but that's impossible. It can't be true.

I push on the door and stumble out.

A small group of people stands in a circle, chatting. The light on the wall is right above their heads, but I still can't see who they are. I hear them laughing, but their faces are all dark.

One of them turns back to me, and I see Raman. Stunned, I stand rooted in the doorway, unable to move and feeling like my eyes are filling with tears. It's him. It's my Raman… It's a dream. It's not true. It can't be true! I saw him lying in the coffin. I saw his pale face! His dead face!

Raman offers me a smile and turns back to the guy he was talking to. No one else even looks at me. I put my hand over my mouth to stop myself from screaming. I need to go home. I need to talk to someone. What the fuck?!

I slowly walk down the stairs, clutching onto the railing with both of my hands. I stare around in panic and hear Raman's voice.

"Miazhevich, where are you going?" He's slowly walking toward me.

I raise my eyes at him. He is looking at me, smiling. I don't see anything else, only his eyes, flickering in the light of the lamp.

Suddenly, I feel immense calmness wash over my body. I breathe out with relief.

"Nowhere, I'm staying."

ABOUT THE AUTHOR

Aldona Martynenka was born and raised in Minsk, Belarus. Growing up in a family of writers, she inherited a deep passion for writing, which began with school writing competitions and essay publications, eventually leading to a career in journalism and non-fiction writing. Influenced by her father, a journalist and music critic, Aldona developed a deep connection with the local music scene, gaining insight into the lives of artists and their behind-the-scenes stories.

Her debut novel, *The Snow Melted in August*, draws inspiration from her personal experiences with loss and drug abuse among loved ones.

Currently residing in Stockholm, Sweden, Aldona works as a product manager while continuing to pursue her passion for writing and working on her next book.